THE ANOUKA CHRONICLES

The Old Oak Tree

Philippa W Joyner

Dear Connoll/
Best wishes,
Pippa.x.

New Generation Publishing

The Tumble

The view was heavenly. Rolling green velvet hills panned out as far as the eye could see with little irregular shaped dirty fluffy cotton wool balls scattered on top, which must be sheep William thought. William leant further forward, and then another inch, and just a little bit more, and then stretched just that little bit higher for a better view. *Crack!* Clutz. He never listened.

The old knobbly branch on which William once stood simply broke. A clean break. William gasped as the air around him whooshed by, his already dishevelled hair flying tall to the sky, or to the earth, it was hard to know what or where. Green leaves from the old oak tree brushed past his face, his twisted feet entangled in twine, and before he could decide which way was up or down, thud. William hit the floor. His face collided with the tree trunk's roots and poor William's forehead span. His vision blurred. Then dark.

"William, William Joy? Can you *hear* me?" a tall elegant figure cried into William's ear. "William. It's Alyssa, can you *see* me?" Alyssa stroked the invalid's head and he mumbled something unintelligible. Not much change there then really.

"Naribu?" William murmured. "Is that you still, Naribu?"

"Let me through, let me through. Out the way. Who is it *this* time, what has the old oak tree done *now*? Anyone hurt? Lately, there seems to be nothing but trouble from this here old tree, it shakes and creaks and seemingly has a complete life of its own. I swear it swung one of its crumbled bark branches at me just this morning as I walked by. And it sniggered. And it sneezed black soot in my direction. There was ample room for me to pass, and not the slightest breeze to move the twigs, but no, I was hit square on the jaw," the complaining, eventful voice of Miss Lovett resounded through the gasps and mutterings in the school playground.

"William Joy fell, Miss," one red-headed boy shouted, pleased he was the first to tell.

"He was right on the top branch, Miss, admiring the view, again. He knows it's dangerous. Then I heard an almighty crack, and William was tumbling through the air," an equally, if not more, red-headed girl added to the commotion.

"William? Nod if you can hear me? Squeeze my hand," Miss Lovett peered into the boy's eyes, sternly, and he sat up.

"Any one got any chocolate?" was William's first words. "I'm starving."

"You're fine, then," Miss Lovett huffed at the boy. "Why do you always create such a fuss, dramas, can't you just keep out of mischief, just for once?" Secretly, Miss Lovett was thankful no harm had come to the boy, and she hurried the school nurse along to press cold paper towels onto William's head. There appeared no swelling, no raised purple pounding bump and equally no cuts or bruises.

"You *are* a brave boy!" Mrs Hill, the plump, ancient bumbling nurse mumbled, pampering the boy who really had no time for her.

"Get off me, I'm fine," William wriggled, grimacing with embarrassment, trying to release himself from the nurse's tight grip. Without success.

"*William!*" Miss Lovett stressed his name. "William! *Enough* of your rudeness. If you're going to climb trees and get into this trouble, all of the time, then you can at least be looked at, again, to make sure you're not knocked out, nearly again, or indeed concussed. One day, I'm sure that will be the case. No doubt about that."

Before brushing down the leafy clothes he had collected on route and standing up, wobbling, he offered a sort of apology. "I'm fine, truly I am," William mumbled in return, fakely, and Miss Lovett could not do much about it. She marched back through the crowds of children, who all had gormless gaping mouths, and William smiled back up at the tree. "Thanks, Naribu," he whispered as he picked white feathers from his ruffled hair, and an owl flew overhead. "Thanks for the insight." The owl winked in reply.

William sat in the shadow the old oak tree cast across the playground. Its heart shaped leaves shed enormous black shapes onto the dusty mud floor and William felt perturbed. He had missed Naribu. His snowy white owl friend had not been in contact forever, and now the Autumn school term had begun, the bird had suddenly revealed himself. He picked up a stick and drew pictures in the chalky ground thinking bravely of Naribu's pressing tale. Untrue, it seemed.

"Hi there, Wills. Are you feeling better?" Alyssa pouted and meandered over, her long legs never seeming to end from where William was sitting. He jumped up. He smoothed his hair. Alyssa turned pink. William had no idea where to put his eyes.

"Oh, yeah, yeah, thanks very much," William replied, trying to sound cool but turning a classic shade of crimson far deeper than Alyssa's ruby tone. He could be polite, if it suited him. But girls, they were another species. Yuk. His heart raced. Alyssa was the eldest and the tallest girl in the school, but she also smelt of lavender and had neat plaits. Another double yuk. He had no time for that prissy stuff. Clean? Pretty? A *girl*? He went purple and his insides twisted at just the thought. Or was it bashful awkwardness which he was yet unable to handle? He threw that thought aside.

But, Alyssa. Alyssa, she had *always* had a soft spot for William ever since his grey school shorts resembled baggy trousers and he had found it really difficult to jump the yellow hurdles at sports day. She had lifted him up, and his ears had shone scarlet. William scribbled out his dust pictures with his moss covered green stick. He kicked the dust everywhere.

"What were you drawing?" Alyssa peered closely and sat cross-legged next to the boy, who now felt like his cheeks were burning with so much embarrassment he did not know how to act. "Well?"

"Oh, nothing, just animals, animals and people," William replied, flippantly, trying to cover up his awkwardness, but it was hard to be cocky to Alyssa. It was okay when it came to Belle, but Alyssa? He was completely at a loss of more intelligent conversation. He coughed. "Animals for the Environment Project this term," William carried on, knowing that would make him seem intelligent. A little. Although his bottom lip did drop, quivering.

Alyssa could quite plainly see that the drawings were much more demonic. "Weird project, if you ask me." Alyssa gave him a sly look. "So what are you doing scrubbing them out? They were good, *really* good. I could have taken a photo for your journal, no? Draw them again." William thought Alyssa was far too insistent, just like a girl to tell him what to do, and although he could not really refuse, he found her interest a bit strange. He picked up his stick, and before the blond girl could bat her eyelashes, William had sketched, again, the most remarkable design in the dry earth. He looked at them, and then at the stick. *Weird! How did I do that?* It wasn't him, for sure.

"Wills, that's awesome!" Alyssa gaped in awe, elbowing the boy in a friendly way and calling him

Wills to make her look popular. "Champion, and your arm, it hardly moved." Alyssa called to her best friend, Imogen, who lumbered over to see. Alyssa peered at the boy. The boy peered back. What *was* he up to? William, he had no idea what he was up to.

"Imy, look at what Wills has drawn in just a few seconds," but as Alyssa spoke her words, William had dashed off. He rarely dashed, he did not know the meaning of the word, but he did it that time. Faultlessly, cowardly, before any more questions were fired at him. He didn't know what to say to one girl, let alone two.

"Belle, it's happened *again*. Anouka has found us." William crashed into his sister who was hanging upside down from the monkey bars. He whispered into his sister's listening ear. Belle's mouth fell open.

Naribu's Tale

"William? Really? Mum's going to go barmy," but Belle's eyes glistened. She was pretty unprincipled when it came to Anouka. "What happened? Is it something to do with that massive uproar earlier, and Miss Lovett?" Belle pointed up into the thick dark branches of the oak tree, and she cowered underneath. She felt its presence. She shuddered. Belle had heard rumours that a boy, in nearly the top class, had, again, climbed to the very top of the oldest tree and just as he was heralding the most fantastic view a great crack of the branch on which he stood had given way causing him to fall the entire height of the tree. She was so embarrassed she could not go and see for she *knew* it would be her brother. But she had heard this boy was absolutely fine, not a scratch on him. Straightaway, she had just carried on hanging precariously from the monkey bars wondering why she had suddenly got so good.

"It was you who fell from right up there, wasn't it?" Belle rolled her eyes. "I bet Mum knows already. It's weird she always seem to know before we even get in the door. And you haven't even got a scratch to show?"

"No. Nothing at all," rattled William. "Naribu saved me."

"Oh *what?*" Belle let her arms go and she fell down, just managing to land feet first. "Naribu? Oh dear, this means the onset of heaps of trouble if he's shown up. How is he?" Belle's face, then realising she had heard her old friend's name, lit up. He was a dear friend, their dear wise old snowy owl, and she had not seen him since their dabbling with the silver chalice. But he always brought trouble.

"Seriously, Belle, he's worried, *really* worried this time," was William's sour reply. He held Belle's gaze. "And I'm *starving.*"

"Why?" implored Belle.

"Because Miss Lovett said I couldn't have any lemon drizzle cake and custard until I stopped getting into fatal scrapes," William hung his head. "It's *so* unfair."

"No, idiot, not why are you hungry, why is Naribu worried? Naribu *never* gets worried. He's far too level-headed. This sounds like my school report is going to be another stinker if Anouka's involved. Seriously, Mum will go up the wall if I'm classed as *"peculiar"* again this term. I read Miss Lovett secretly sent this home, and it wasn't even report time. *"Belle is an exceptionally clever individual, but she keeps being late for class and submitting rather bizarre homework. Is she quite alright?"* She frowned and stared at her brother, who just seemed to be sniffing out the kitchen aromas.

"Mmm, cherry roulade and chocolate sauce..." mumbled William. His nose started to move towards the smell whilst his feet stayed put on the floor.

"William, do you know why Naribu is here? Do you? *William!"* but Belle had no idea why she thought her brother could help when food was around. "Why is he worried? Is it really bad in Anouka? Has something happened to his tree home?"

The kitchen windows slammed shut. A scowling cook shook her head William's way. William jumped. "Oh, no, oh...Naribu? Oh, no, not just his tree home, but..." William slowly surveyed his surroundings to make sure no one was listening. He leant in close to his sister. No one else should know. Only Alyssa was still close by. She was chatting and laughing with Imy who gasped and nodded in reply to her best friend's questioning. Alyssa opened her satchel, and Imy peered inside. Imy looked anxious. Her homework was not obviously as well presented as Alyssa's. "Why can't I just have a taster of cherry roulade and chocolate sauce?"

"*WILLIAM!* Get your mind out the oven!" Belle raged. Mrs Joy was going to string her up alive if her still life fruit bowl suddenly turned out to be a dragon eating owl; again. "Anouka? What's up?"

"...it's not just Naribu in trouble, but the entire grounds on which his home now grows." William looked upwards towards the ancient oak tree; he was seemingly talking in some kind of trance. Belle squinted at her brother's weirdness. The tree creaked under some unseen pressure.

"What do you mean?" Belle looked anxious. She followed her brother's gaze to the tops of the branches. "*This* tree? This old oak tree which has been here for centuries? Naribu actually lives *here*, and it's in danger? Oh God, I'm so not going to get an A* for Art this term if my paintings start to go up in smoke again. The entire easel where I was quite plainly striking a pose of pineapples and quince in a basket just shot into flames just missing Conniving Cat. Shame that. I was down-graded to a C minus just for bad behaviour and an unwillingness to own up to having matches in my bag, despite my work leaving everyone else for dust all year. I swear it was Cat. She even kicked the matchbox out of view."

"Belle, shut *up!* We're *all* in danger, not just your pineapples and quince," whispered William, his voice undeniably shaking as he spoke. "Belle, listen, I fell not because I was being foolish and stupid, again, and leaning out far too far, which, okay, I was, but the whole oak tree shook from the roots upwards and I lost my footing. It pushed me. This tree actually shoved me off. As I tumbled, Naribu flew hooting towards me. Catching me in his wide white wing span, he retold a terrible story. A Black Witch, Xavishum, arrived in Anouka last night and her presence is so strong she can destroy this tree and all it holds. It's the hub of Anouka. Naribu's home is about to disappear, disappear completely into the earth. To dust. To nothing."

"Along with my oil paintings," Belle scorned, pulling at her rat's tailed hair. "I'm not having that."

"Apparently the main door to this greying world lies secretly, somewhere here, in its trunk, and if Xavishum escapes out from within, our school is doomed."

"Our school? It can get out here?" Belle threw back her hair, but it just stayed, knotted, where it was. "But William, only a chosen few can see Anouka and its people and its powers. How can a Black Witch destroy our school?"

"Who do you think I am? God? Naribu? I don't know!" William kicked at the earth with his toes. He zoned out again. He looked possessed. "Naribu told me that Xavishum arrived from another part of Anouka. A dark side which was sealed irreversibly with her goblins and sprites locked away many centuries back. But Xavishum found a way through. Now she's here and she wants our school as her preying ground. Apparently one of her servant goblins has already broken free of this old oak tree. He's somewhere in the school, disguised. Xavishum has far stronger powers than Naribu can ever possess. She can turn our world upside down."

"*Don't* scuff your shoes, William."

Angus Moon and Alyssa Fellstrop

"Blimey..." Belle muttered as she walked, alone, across the grass, scuffing *her* shoes. But her voice was hidden. The school bell was ringing for the afternoon.

"William, what is *your* answer?" Miss Lovett questioned the mesmerised boy as the white sun streaked through the glass panes. "William, are you *with* us?" and a chalk board duster flew across the classroom to land in the distracted boy's lap. Chalk flew into his face. William jumped. It was evident he could not concentrate at all during science.

"Forty eight," William shouted. "If there are eight large rainbows shining through this arc, and we increase them six fold, there will be forty eight."

"Correct, boy. You *were* listening, strange that, despite gazing out through the window." Miss Lovett glared at the child. His eyes were clouded over. "What is out *there*?" Miss Lovett frowned, and seemingly slid towards the sashes, inquisitively, to peer out. The class jumped as she slammed the blinds shut.

"No one, I mean nothing, nothing at all. No one out there." William put up his hand for distraction to answer question two which had been chalked up on the blackboard.

"Yes, William Joy, *again*. Does no one else have the answers today?" Miss Lovett looked annoyed. "Go on."

"Sunlight and rainwater all help in a process called photosynthesis." William tried hard to redeem himself just in time as the bell rang out for the end of class. Miss Lovett praised the heavens. William looked outside. Naribu winked back through the tiniest of slats created by one misplaced window blind. It was a wink of help.

***

"So Belle, as I looked around at the view and I saw the smoke spiralling high into the air from Dad's bonfire, I heard a massive loud rumble and the entire oak tree trembled. The acorns, partly grown and still green in their small round cases, tumbled from the branches around me and a shadow of a small person loomed larger and larger from below. The shadow spread across the field and through all the boys playing football. It turned the ground dark but no one else stopped in their tracks except me. Then a new boy appeared at the school gate, seemingly lost. I didn't recognise his face, drawn and pale it was with a sprinkling of hazel brown freckles. Then I thought of Naribu's tale of the goblin disguised and roaming free. Do you think this new boy could be him? It's all a bit odd." William dragged his heels.

"Don't scuff your heels, William," Belle ground her teeth.

"Why not? *You* do things like that! Your hairbrush is disgusting, and you think Mum will buy you another now all the prongs have flown out?" William retorted.

"They're not prongs, they're bristles, and it's my brush, so stop snooping around!" Belle ignored her brother. Her nose pointed to the sky.

"Whatever, I don't care about your hairbrush. I just want you to stop ordering me around. What *is* it with girls?" William spoke to himself really.

"Anyway…" Belle changed the subject. "It can't, it can't possibly be Angus Moon. He's just too timid and polite it's not true. The new boy, today, he looks a bit of a wimp."

"I know, it was so embarrassing at javelin, he practically got lost behind it!" William cackled.

"That's mean…" Belle flung her overly-sized bag over her shoulder, narrowly missing her brother's head.

"Idiot…" William carried on walking, trailing behind and occasionally looking back at that old oak tree. It was getting larger, bushier, more twisted and evil in shape. Thin charcoal smoke rose from its topmost branch, and…and was that a squirrel in flames teetering on the edge of life and death? The boy turned away. "Mind you, it would send anyone looking for a grimacing escapee off the scent for sure. Send a nimble, bony boy into our world. Naribu told of the Black Witch and her servants able to turn other worlds not part of Anouka to shame. The Black Witch can perish all in her path and she will use all her powers to do so." William's mind tampered with the worst scenario.

"You *really* think Angus Moon is the Black Witch's accomplice?" Belle ridiculed the idea. Although she shook. "A disguised goblin? He's a wimp!"

"Why not? Maybe," William muttered, quickening his pace up through Church Meadow. "I'm a genius, but I also look gormless at times."

***

Angus Moon scuffed the fronts of his shoes as he slowly traipsed back from school after his first, overwhelmingly unpleasant, day. It was so grey. But now, as he sauntered along, the sun's rays were becoming hotter and stronger. He liked the warmth on his face, but it was a bit weird the heat was getting more and more powerful as the sun should be going down. Never mind, it was so much more pleasant than what he was used to. He sighed. He missed his old friends.

"Arbrooth is just such a *long* way away," Angus's accent floated about his head on the gentle breeze. He continued to scuff his feet, harder, until one shoe practically fell apart altogether. He sighed, again, aloud, to himself. The wind picked up and blew Angus's thick strands of hair quite tall and he held his head up high to the welcome draught. "It's nice here though too," Angus tried to bolden up.

The trail of the wind and Angus's words carried far. Angus turned into the open gate leading to the village stream and the pond. The water in the pond seemed wild, but to Angus it seemed quite normal. He was more than used to troubled weather where he was from. He was also used to a long walk home after school and his feet could not help but want to discover his new home. He still scuffed his toes, though. "I do *like* it here, I think, and I will *try* to make friends. I have to really, I really need to fit in tomorrow otherwise I'll be doomed." The new boy chuckled to himself and stared into the torrent of what was really just a pond. "What was *THAT*?" Angus choked on his apple and leapt up high backwards, falling right over.

The air seemed warm, and William now walked ahead of his sister. Fast. It was untypically William, but he could not help it. There was a pull, like an invisible piece of string was choking him from the neck downwards and reeling him further and further, and not even in quite the right direction.

"Wait, wait for *me!*" Belle grimaced as the breeze picked up. "Why are you always so bolshy?"

"Sssssssssssh…" William held up his hand as if to halt an army.

"Don't you sssssssssssh *me!* Cretin!" Belle retorted, tossing her hair. The mass of knotted locks just flicked up and then back down in a thick clump. She ran to catch up with her brother. Her open bag, stuffed full, swung out behind. What a mess. She was just about to swing her hefty lump of belongings full of unclean paint brushes and hardback art books at William screaming "Cretin, cretin…" when William glared at her, his eyes bulging, flagging her outburst down.

"Shut *up*, Belle, I meant be quiet. Why are you such an idiot? Stupid girls." William squinted about, cautiously. "I heard a voice, a lonesome old dialect of a voice. Really odd. The wind brought it to me, but the tone is not quite right." William frowned, he peered around, and he strained his ears to try and understand the words more clearly, but, as he listened more intently to the foreign tone, his mouth fell open. He saw the new boy, Angus, fly through the air. Angus shot higher and higher with nothing beneath his flapping trousers, the tops of them falling down, and his bony fingers trying to keep them up. Belle saw his underpants, chequered and red, and started to laugh and point before she realised what was actually happening. Then, Angus tumbled to the floor with a painful clatter. His eyes bulged, as his bottom hit the deck. *THUD!* Wet grasses and sharp pebbles flew everywhere. Angus rubbed his head. Belle heard his moaning and ran to help. The reeds surrounding the pond rustled to themselves, and then crept back as if to hide. A dark shadow retracted deeper beneath the soil.

"It's the new boy! Hey, new boy, are you okay?" Belle ran towards Angus's bruised muddy body.

"Belle, *Belle* come back, what are you doing?" William screamed at his sister as she kicked off her black patent shoes and ran through the now dry grasses to see if Angus was hurt. "Belle, I saw him *fly...*" William whispered into the distance, but his words were taken by the sudden gusts, and his flighty sister was too far away and certainly not listening to any warnings of danger. "Belle, that new boy could be the Black Witch's goblin accomplice?"

Angus just stared back at him.

"The Black Witch's goblin *who*?" Angus repeated back to William and sat up. He had heard. "Me?" Angus laughed. "Is that a new pantomime at school? Arbrooth, my home town, had an awesome panto group. I always played the chimney sweep, can't think why I was never given a more evil or a more funny role?" Angus shook his head. He ruffled his bedraggled hair, that looked as if it was always only ever that way, and stood up.

"Your voice is...weird." Belle frowned, but liked Angus. "Where are you from?"

"Belle! Belle, stand back." William stared wide-eyed at his sister. "We had better be off home now, yes Belle?" and he nodded his chin upwards at Angus. Angus looked unassuming, pale and freckled, and a thin lad. But he was still unsure. An overly large newt ran up William's inside trouser leg. He slapped it off.

"Why?" Angus replied, tipping his head downwards. "Why do you have to go now? We've only just met." He leant forwards towards Belle to whisper in her ear, but William dragged her away.

"Leave her alone! Don't touch my sister," barked William, uncharacteristically protective of his younger sibling. "So, tell us then..." he continued, pushing his sister behind his back.

"Tell you what?" Angus's voice sounded peculiar once more. "Who do you think I am?"

"Tell us where you came from?" demanded William, still gripping his sister's wrist.

"Let me go, William, you're hurting me. Did you not take *any* notice in that bullying session last week?" Belle tried to pull her arm away, but her brother's grasp was too tight.

"Did the Black Witch send you? If she did, your colony, they shan't win you know. We *will* defeat you." William stamped his left foot forward as if it was a threat.

"I'm from Arbrooth," Angus answered. He looked at William, carefully. "Who in God's name do you think I am?" He was now quite enjoying this. "I'm just a boy."

"I suppose that's the dark side, Arbrooth? The locked away world which Anouka shut out centuries ago? The world where the Black Witch roams? I *know* she has escaped. I *know* she plans to turn our school into her deep dark preying ground, a school to teach spells and turn the sun to ice and the children into slaves. Naribu told me the tale. I know one of her goblin accomplices is now disguised and roams free. It's you, isn't it?" William scowled, and not even Belle had ever seen her brother so crazed.

"Arbrooth? It's in Scotland. I'm Scottish." Angus smiled. "Sorry if that's not exciting enough. What a weird village. I think I'm going to like it here," Angus announced, politely. "BUT WHAT IS THAT?" And he ducked. An enormous crested wave from the pond turned into a gigantic swell, and as the tip broke, the most repugnant creature with green warts, a pointed hooked nose with flared nostrils, and sharp fingernails covered in algae giving off the most repulsive stench, emerged from the waters. It fled.

"What *was* that?" cried Angus in despair. "I think I preferred Arbrooth!" Angus continued to lie dead flat on the floor, algae dripping from his ears and brown acidic water filling up his shoes, and then the soles clean fell off. "Mum's gonna kill me."

As the water continued to crash down, William dragged his sister and the dripping, insipid, stinking Scottish boy out of its path. The creature zipped through the clouds and disappeared back inside the old oak tree. Thick black sludge slopped on its trunk.

"That, *that* must have been the Black Witch's goblin accomplice, for sure." William's jaw dropped as he pointed into the incinerated distance where the old oak tree stood. "Sorry, mate." And he held out his hand to shake Angus's. But Angus, he was out cold.

Lightning cracked. Fire surrounded the old oak tree. William tugged his raincoat over the three dumbstruck heads as they huddled together until they reached home. Only two pairs of legs were actually walking though.

***

"Yes, William, I *have* heard, so there's no need to try and worm your way out of it this time, again." Mrs Joy flung her tea towel over her shoulder and pulled the children indoors. "Oh, *three* of you? Are you quite al*right*?" She peered into Angus's eyes. "Apparently not." She tugged the raincoat free and flung it over the same shoulder as the tea towel which in turn became wetter for drying. "Come in, come in, out the storm. It blew up from nowhere. Anything to do with *you*, William?" Mrs Joy scrutinised her son, and in turn he just pretended not to hear and shoved his nose further towards the oven door. Something was happening in there.

Continuing to roughly towel dry the three heads, which inevitably got wetter as the tea towel was wringing itself out Angus swore, Mrs Joy huffed. "Where *did* that downpour come from? It was glorious sunshine when I pulled eggs from chicken behinds, and then that wind which whipped up knocked me for six, I nearly dropped the lot. And did you smell that tremendous stink of sewage? Never before has a storm caught me so unawares. Hello, there. What's your name?" and the tall lady, a Mother who chattered incessantly without fail, turned to Angus and towel-dried the new boy's head so hard that he fell into the inglenook fireplace.

That woke Angus completely. "*Me?* Me? Angus. I'm Angus Moon," Angus's teeth chattered even though his back seemed to be getting hotter and hotter. He continued smiling and smelling at the same time, but it was not just biscuits baking in the oven. Angus's nostrils detected another, less pleasant, smell. "My *jumper!* My jumper's on fire!!! What? My Mum is actually going to lock me in the cellar now, with the dog! The dog is *always* in the cellar." Wisps of burning wool filled the kitchen and Mrs Joy opened the window.

"Thank the Lord my biscuits aren't too burnt," she sang. Angus just looked at her. And then at the others. A wisp of blackening smoke appeared through a crack in the oven door, and just a small burning smell went up their noses.

"Are you all mad? My jumper!" Angus grabbed the soaked tea towel and started to smack himself on the back, oh and then on his bottom as the fire had taken hold there as well. "My trousers now. My entire school uniform has been burnt to a crisp!" But no one seemed to really care. "You *are* all mad."

"My gingerbreads!" Mrs Joy grabbed back her tea towel and whisked the ever so slightly tinged oddly shaped gingerbread people from the hot oven and threw the tray onto the rustic tiled work surface. "If only I could remember to set my oven timer, the biscuits for the Women's Institute wouldn't always be so over-crunchy. Never mind, would you like to taste them?" She shoved the plate of burning hot gingerbreads under Angus's nose.

"I, I suppose so…" Angus mumbled, thinking he had no other choice.

"Honest truths, please. Are they really too hard and tasting of charcoal to offer to the highest members of the WI tonight?"

"They're lovely," Belle replied. The inglenook roared.

"To die for," William continued, pulling a face as he grabbed Angus from the cushioned wooden rocking chair and up the cottage staircase, three stories high, to his shared bedroom. Belle followed. The inglenook's flames took over the kitchen, and Mrs Joy scraped the morsels into the bin.

"Blatant fibbers," Mrs Joy smiled.

"She's, er, nice," Angus could not think what on earth to say. He sat with William and Belle, crossed legged on the crimson fur rug in the largest room in the house, the attic room shaped just so. His clothes hung in shreds around his ashen body.

"You're a bit, er, pale," Belle picked at the new boy's brittle clothes. "Sorry about the shock, it's always like that here."

"I'm always pale." Angus picked at his jumper sleeves; unravelling the wool so far that one arm actually fell off. "Oh." It looked like Angus needed a bit of help. "I'm from Scotland. We're all pale there. Not much sun, but at least my clothes stay on! I'm burnt to nothing!"

"That's Mum," William snorted, picking hard gingerbread crumbs from his teeth. "Sorry about that."

"What was all that about?" Angus tried to forget about what might happen when he rocked up home that night, and he spoke up. He sounded muffled. One of the biscuits had hardened onto his gums.

"Just our Mum. I tried to tell you but she kept just drying your hair. Are you okay? Your forehead, it looks a bit sore. She is one to talk and scurry you along. I used to barely have my socks pulled up and she would be hurrying me out the stable door to school…in my younger years." William tapped his fingers on the carpet.

"It still happens…" Belle coughed out her reply.

"No, I didn't mean your Mum, mine's the same, I'm sure they *all* are. Well, I had hoped it wasn't just mine. No, I meant the pond, that…well…that creature from the pond. What was it? I saw its reflection in the water as I peered in, just before you came along, although I have to admit at first I thought it was a large rough toad beneath the reefs. Something English." Angus threw William a half chiselled smirk. William did not look amused. "Was that your Black Witch's goblin accomplice, then?"

"I dunno." William was in a mood. "I guess, but she's not *my* witch. I thought *you* were it, that accomplice."

"Is that why you've got that long mooooooody face, William?" Belle poked him, hard, in the ribs. "Because you haven't captured it?"

"Get lost."

"Did you think you'd struck gold? Caught it?" Belle nudged her brother and screwed up her face in his direction. "Hahahaha, William!" She stuck out her tongue.

"I said *GET LOST!* And I saw that." William turned his back to both of them.

"He's in a mood," Belle whispered to Angus, loudly, cupping her hand so her brother could hear.

"GET LOST!!!!!"

"We're trying to banish her back to the dark side of Anouka," Belle let Angus in, and William gradually turned his sly glance back.

"Anouka?" Angus looked completely lost. His parents had come to a rather mad English village. He thought Arbrooth was quirky, but Hollingbourne was much more awry with strangeness. "Anouka, I thought I was in Hollingbourne?"

"Oh, you are," Belle answered quickly.

"I'm totally lost now."

"Anouka..." Belle looked around her attic room. It creaked. "Anouka, it's a parallel world," Belle mouthed her words.

"I can't hear you. What *are* you talking about?" Angus tried to lip read. "Heaven's above! Arbrooth, take me back! Rain, storms, floods, I'll gladly take it all!" But, at that point, Mrs Joy rapped on the attic door.

"Stinging nettle and carotene stew, and it is ready now, and I mean, only NOW before it boils to nothing." Then, the voice of madness, it disappeared.

"Brace yourself!" William turned his warning to Angus, but Angus had already decided for himself to be pretty vigilant if he was to survive.

"Anouka?" Angus whispered as he gathered up his school books and re-ruffled his hair for the third time that afternoon. Belle was counting.

"Come on, the unpalatable pickings will be boiling over by now." Belle pushed the two, less than eager, boys further towards the attic room door, herding them along like sheep.

William leant towards Angus. "Now I have Belle to rush me. I think my Mum gave up years ago!" William sniggered. Angus winked back, for he knew the boy was trying to make up.

"Oy, I heard that, cretin! Double carotene with spinach purée for you, I'm telling!" and Belle threw her creased up but completed poem entitled *'Autumn Days'* at her brother. "I bet you haven't even begun yours, have you? I heard Isla and Robyn tittering in the corner by the old oak tree today swapping ideas on, what was the topic?" Belle squinted to remember the girls' conversation.

William shook his head at his sister. She knew he didn't really care.

"...oh yes, *'Trees through the Ages. What Tales do they Tell?'*" Belle felt secretly pleased she had not only finished her homework but she knew all about William's too. "Oh, then Isla stepped back and obviously took a marvellous photo for her Autumn Project. She looked so accomplished as she looked at the results on her camera. Mind you, her jaw dropped at one picture, for sure, as she took a quick glance back at the tree then ran after Robyn through the school gate, and I've never seen Alyssa look so fierce. She reprimanded Isla a bit too much, for running in school grounds I guess. Oh yes, then Alyssa tried to confiscate Isla's camera. I thought that was a bit harsh, even for head girl. She's only ever been nice to you, William?" Belle ranted on.

"Competition for who can talk longest without gasping for air?" Angus teased, shaking his head in William's direction and getting praise for it. Angus tickled Belle's bare shoulders. "Belle or your Mum, William?"

"*Jerk.*" Belle stared at her brother and strode downstairs. "He's your NBF now? You're *so* of the moment." Belle stomped. She was annoyed. *She* was the one who had helped Angus, and now William had taken him on. "If it wasn't for *me*, Angus would still be lying in a ditch. Wet. Hurt. *Dead!* At least *I* think it's odd Alyssa trying to confiscate Isla's camera, just for running?" she spoke to herself. Angus heard.

"Rools are Rools," Angus interrupted, baring his broadest Scottish accent.

"*You!* You're just cocky. Wish I'd left you there now." Belle fell, sulkily, down each step, her slender heels sounding like a herd of elephants. She slumped. Her feet scuffed on the carpet stairwell.

"*Don't* scuff your tights, Belle." William took great joy in that. But perhaps Alyssa did know something more.

Belle unhunched her shoulders. A little. "William, do you think Isla's camera took a photograph of something it should not have, part of the old oak tree that only a snapshot in time could give away? A *warning?* Isla's face was totally random, and grey as anything when she saw what her camera had captured." Belle sat bolt upright. "Shall we pay her a visit?"

However, just as Belle mentioned Isla's name a great darkening wind slammed the attic door tight shut, rattling the walls so much a picture fell clean off smashing to the floor. Glass splinters shot everywhere.

The reverberations penetrated the room heaving all in its path, and Belle slipped down three steps twisting her ankle. She grabbed the hand rail. Bits of paint came off in her hand. "Our room, it's falling apart," she cried as she hung onto what was left of the bannister. It just crumbled more and more.

Mrs Joy, abysmally unaware, called from the steaming kitchen. "*EAT* your soup before its valuable nutrients are washed away…" but her hollering was lost to the lurid, gloomiest shadow cast into the attic, and the gnarling ugly goblin from the pond pressed its gruesome face up at the old sash window howling and squirming to get in.

Belle rattled the attic room door as hard as she could. "It must know. That thing *must* know we are onto it." Belle continued to shake the round brass door handle but it would not budge. "It's normally loose, just falls open, it's not working, *why…..are…..you…..stuck?"* she cried, wrenching the handle as hard as she could. The dark shadow of the ugly goblin hammering at the window cast the entire attic room a raven atrocity in colour, but just as Belle became utterly exhausted, panicking to open the door, it flew back off its hinges. Mrs Joy stood the other side; cabbage leaf shreds and old purple curly kale hanging from her hair. Her apron was tied up all wrong.

"What *is* all this racket? This door will come clean off its hinges one day if you continue to mess around with it so fiercely. Oh, it has. Honestly...*time* and *time* again."

Belle turned her head back up into the attic. It lay bright and the early evening sun had made the entire wall deep orange in colour. She stared at the window. It was calm outside. The picture, shattered, sucked its glass shards back in place, and the room lay silent. Eerie. "Get out of our faces, cretin," Belle whispered to the long gone beast in the silent room.

"Belle! Leave your brother be!" Mrs Joy's words flew up the stairs whilst she carried on down. "Of all the worldly worlds, why is she sooooo reckless, and what with a new boy here, really."

Angus tried to help. "Lovely up here, Mrs Joy." He still picked at his teeth. His gums were now a little raw, and his head, blimey, his head from the towel, it was throbbing. He called further. "Nice, errr, smell."

"Yes," Mrs Joy replied. "Soup. Yes, yes, yes, the views are great too, most of the time." Her last words drifted off. All Angus could really think about was the sickly dreadful goblin who had filled the window pane just before. "Are you alright now, child?"

"Never better," he lied.

"Oh, I nearly forgot. Alyssa's downstairs." And Mrs Joy disappeared. From the kitchen, she shouted. "She's brought you a photo, William. Apparently you sketched a zany, peculiarly amazing design? Into the dusty earth at school today? Your talents are ripening, but can you show them in the classroom next time, please? That would be good. Oh, and Alyssa wants to give you this snapshot for your *Journal*. What's that all about, please? It's all a bit secret; she would *not* let me see. Hope it's not another of those weird exploding toad things again. I couldn't bear to have to go see Miss Lovett and explain why I, apparently, let you keep seventeen toads in the pond to breed." Mrs Joy was heard puffing as she stirred the pot. Her brow perspired. The soup was putty, again. "She, Alyssa, said she had to come right away and let you know. Sorry dear, sorry to talk about you when you're standing right there." Alyssa held her nose. "Quite persistent she is this head girl." Mrs Joy winked at the very wet looking girl dripping on her kitchen floor. "Dear, my dear, pass me your coat, and go on, go on into the dining room, there's plenty to go around."

Alyssa snubbed her nose. She had no intention of eating that slop, but she sat down, on the edge of the closest chair hugging her bag tightly. "I don't want secrets and goings on outside, I'd rather you just stayed indoors." Mrs Joy held her head out towards the corridor. "Williaaaaaaaaaaaaam, she's waiting at the table. Well, come on! Oh my dear Lord..." The ladle was cemented in.

"Alyssa?" Belle waited at the foot of the attic staircase. "That's a bit of a coincidence? First the Black Witch's accomplice appears and disappears, then Alyssa turns up."

"And?" William reddened, casting Belle aside. He walked ahead. "Hi *Al.*"

"You fickle old..." Belle pushed past Angus and, pretending to be carefree, tumbled with laughter into the dining room and collapsed into her chair. "*Al?* Idiot," she uttered at her brother.

"Hi *Belle,*" Alyssa eyed up the little sister.

"Hi, *Al!*" Belle replied.

"Hello Alyssa," Angus smiled. "What brings you up here? Quite a walk from your cottage, isn't it?"

Alyssa returned Angus's smile, but she looked around, sceptically. Something was not quite right about the girl. She seemed tense, tetchy. "How do you know where I live?"

"Oh, I saw you across the…pond." Angus's nose curled up. "Did *you* bring that awful sewers smell in? It's gross!"

"Nearly ready, wholesome this will be." Mrs Joy tried to add goat's milk to the ever thickening gruel in her pot.

"The pond?" Alyssa sat upright.

"Yeah, yeah," Belle butted in. "Been there, done that, Angus is *not* the Black Wit….."

"*BELLE!*" William kicked his sister.

Alyssa sipped her soup. In pretence. They all sipped their soup. In pretence. William poured his in the spider plant. It died, immediately. The soup seemed to be getting hotter and hotter, not cooler. Steam arose from all of the bowls, and no one could barely put the tip of their tongue on a mere teaspoonful let alone gulp down huge ladles like Mrs Joy was encouraging with arms flailing about in the doorway. It solidified. The soup turned green, a disgusting rotten algae colour, and Alyssa coughed to clear her voice. She leant in. Belle rolled her eyes. Alyssa was such a pretence.

"I've come to warn you," Alyssa mumbled quietly though her cupped hands.

"You're always crying for attention, you're so false, you with your long legs and your tangle-free hair and your pouting..." Belle chaised back and mimicked Alyssa.

"Whatever, *RosaBELLA*," Alyssa sniped back

"Don't you call me that, it's just *Belle* nowadays."

"Get lost, Belle. *Warn* us? What do you mean?" William lay across the entire table.

Alyssa leant closer still until her nose practically brushed William's. "As you know, the Black Witch has escaped from dark Anouka. She is cursed."

"*We* know. But how do *you* know, Alyssa? Are you alright? You look drained." William started to feel sorry for her until Belle kicked his ankle. She glared at her brother.

"You know when you hated Angus, William? Well...THAT," Belle uttered. "Do you get me?"

"Blimey, Belle, just eat your soup." But he did not let on that perhaps Alyssa could be pretending. A trap. She had come in at the same time their foul dinner had arrived. "Zip it," was his only reply to Belle.

"Cretin, again."

"Listen," Alyssa whispered. "You don't understand. I know Anouka too. I once had what I thought was a dream but I had actually fallen into Anouka; the cusp between the light and the dark. Naribu helped me to escape."

Belle's eyes focused a little more. "Have you been spying on us? You *have*, haven't you?"

"If you must know, *Rosabella*, I fell into Anouka's dark side last summer, and the Black Witch made me promise to let her into our world through a great portal in the old oak tree. She made me promise to help her escape Anouka, to roam in a real world of humans. I had to say yes, she had her goblins at my throat, but I have *never* gone back to help. Now one of her accomplices has found his way into our world and it surely won't be long before she does too. She's gonna kill me." A large tear fell from Alyssa's eyes. "Here…" Alyssa reached deep into her bag.

"Get back, *Wills*," Belle lurched forward to drag her brother away, but she only succeeded in scratching his arm. "Don't fall for *her*." Belle flicked a solid lump of soup at the girl. It did not splatter as it had no liquid in it at all, but it did smack Alyssa right in the centre of her forehead, then the lump slopped down into Alyssa's own bowl. The bowl cracked at the side, and some of the mixture oozed out onto the mat.

"Belle, you idiot..." William pushed her away. Belle's chair wobbled, and if she had not grabbed hold of the tablecloth she would have smacked onto the floor. Alyssa smashed her fist onto the tablecloth. It stayed put. Belle scowled. Alyssa pulled out a picture. William's simple picture. "Dumb-brain personified." William gawped.

"William. Look in the background. There's the portal, that gaping black hole, getting wider and wider each day." And as William peered closer in, he could see the deepening crevice whirl and spit, and he could hear the pounding of feet and the chanting of weird voices. "Isla took an identical photo just this afternoon. I tried to retrieve her camera. If she sees the portal she will be involved, like us, and surely be in grave danger. The Black Witch is certainly after me. She cursed me. I didn't return as promised. I've been scared out my wits for months. As soon as I left my cottage this evening her goblin accomplice followed my quickening steps. I could see him in my shadows. I hid by the stream and I saw him crashing at your attic window. I think he was after me. I have betrayed the Black Witch, and her goblin accomplice has entered our world to get me." Another huge tear plopped into Alyssa's empty soup bowl; its remnants now dripping all over the carpet. Alyssa could not stop crying. "You must help me, and help yourselves. We have to stop the Black Witch and her evil servants."

"Trickster..." Belle retorted.

"William, Rosabella, you have barely begun your tea. No friends if you chatter all night. I'm not getting a visit, am I, from the school? Are you baking up inedible sausage pickle recipes again, pickles which turned Hubert completely turquoise? I do hope not. His Mum didn't stop sending me doctor's bills for a month." Mrs Joy continued to peel a never ending heap of oddly shaped home grown red carrots and to chop muddy leeks for the next meal. "Same time tomorrow, Alyssa?" There was no reply.

"Who *is* the goblin accomplice then, know-all, *Al*?" Belle asked Alyssa, still hardened to the head girl's plea.

"We need to find out, Rosabella." Alyssa pushed back her chair and whispered. "I've said too much already." She disappeared into the night.

"Oh, bye then dear." Mrs Joy was in a world of her own. "No gratitude these days. *Rosabella*, look at my CARPET!" Belle had gone too.

Myriad

Art was his worst subject. It wasn't to say that William wasn't any good at drawing, it was more pure boredom. He thought it was a waste of his precious time. Class after class Miss Terrine just rolled her eyes and rapped her disgusting yellowed cracked fingernails on William's desk. "William Joy, it's been nearly an hour and your paper is still, errr, blank. What *have* you been doing all lesson?"

"Nothing, Miss..." William always sat up and answered, realizing that was *exactly* what he had been doing. Nothing. What he had meant, each time, to say was *"Oh, it's nothing, Miss, I'm getting to it, just working which is better to sketch; The Coconut Island or The Landscape with Fruit in the Background...?"* but the bell always cut him short.

"Excuses, excuses, that's all I ever seem to hear from you. Can't you just *get on* with whatever you're drawing, quickly? Life doesn't wait for *you*, dear boy. Seize *it* by the horns, take a punt and throw yourself in..." Miss Terrine bent towards the boy that particular morning. She was so tall it seemed to take an eternity for her pointed gaunt face to reach William's, but once

44

their noses were almost touching and her body was stooped so low he thought she could not possibly ever get back up, she whispered "…before *it* seizes you. Get it?" Miss Terrine stood back up. Effortlessly. "I said, *GET IT*, boy? Well?"

"Yes, Miss." William had no idea what she was going on about. She'd always been weird. Weirder than Belle, but at least Belle didn't stink of old coffee.

From his art room desk, William could see that old oak tree. It was surely growing broader, and thicker and darker into the most encrusted brown barked tree he had ever seen, but no one else seemed to even notice. The oak tree was losing precious green leaves by the day, as if it could not control its demise. The tree, or its possessor, seemed to have enforced a life of its own. William inhaled to calm himself down, but felt anxious inside. Miss Terrine stared at him. Her eyes did not blink once.

"Weirdo," William huffed under his breath as he tried to sketch, his pencil barely touching the surface of his blank white paper. It had actually started to turn yellow. Then, *clonk!* William sat bolt upright. Miss Terrine poked her nose in William's direction once more to see what was the commotion and then she cocked her head like a Great Dane to one side to try and spy on him. She shook her head and pointed her magically ever-increasing sharpened pencil his way. She shook it at him. "What are you up to? Can't you pick on someone else?" William spent most of the morning casting aspersions her way, and he kept his head low, still muttering. He started to feel a little uncomfortable.

Then *CLONK*, again! "What *is* that?" William looked around. He saw nothing. Then a third time, *CLONK*, and this time, a little sharp-pointed pebble hit the boy on the brow right between his bushy eyebrows. "Ouch! *Who* threw that?" he glared at Conniving Cat, who had been moved into his class for good behaviour. "Loser." Conniving Cat grinned back, then carried on with her nearly bare sketch of her favourite Rock Star.

William looked back down at his still empty page. The clock above Miss Terrine's head clicked to a quarter to twelve. He only had 15 minutes before lunchtime. Then *CLONK!* A fourth pebble hit his left ear, it scraped past his lobe, and this time William stood up. "*RIGHT*, who keeps throwing pebbles at me?" He searched the room, scrutinising the sea of faces who just stared, dumbfounded, back in his direction. "Come on?

46

Own up!" William asked in the same questioning tone, and he rubbed his forehead, but at the same time he felt a tiny tug at his left shoelace. Slowly pushing back his stool and peering downwards, squinting, what he saw made him immediately pay attention.

"At last, William Joy. Something to say? A masterpiece to share with the class, well?" Miss Terrine's usual high-pitched voice reverberated through the air. "You *do* appear to look rather excited. The fruit bowl in your still life picture must be pleasing? Well? Have you actually produced something in the nick of time?" Miss Terrine asked, inquiringly, and then the tall thin lady, with a tight bun securing her wiry grey hair, rose tall from her chair, as if she was never ever going to stop standing up, at the front of the classroom and walked down the central aisle towards the boy. She seemed to take forever. William could not bear it. Her eyes did not leave his perplexed gaze. William just sat in his chair, moving further and further back as if it surely should tip backwards soon.

William coughed, and felt a little tickle run up his leg. From the tips of his toes, and all the way up the length of his shin, over his knee and scrabble up his grey-clothed thigh ran a pair of quick nimble legs until they found their way across his brown leather belt and hopped onto his rather blank stark white sheet of art paper.

Miss Terrine grew nearer. William gulped. He stared at his non eventful piece of white paper. Then his eyes fell open, and both irises popped out on stalks. The entire class stared at William. William stared at his paper, and his grey-skinned face broke into a smile of amazement.

"*Let* me see your apparent genius sketch, William Joy," Miss Terrine demanded as she bent down and down and down further from her great skinny height, balancing on her high-heeled orange mules, and pushing her narrow pink-rimmed glasses onto the tip of her long bony nose. Her eyes then also grew wide in alarm.

"*WILLIAM JOYYYYYYY!* Your drawing is an absolute *MARVEL*. Did someone *else* do this for you, boy?" She looked William up and down.

"No, Miss," William lied.

"This pencil sketch is by far the best I have *ever* seen from you, ever seen from *anyone*, in many a year in my classroom." And Miss Terrine slapped the boy so hard on his back that his blueberries from breakfast came straight back up. He choked. "Now, now, don't get all over-emotional on me, boy. Wipe those tears." And Miss Terrine used the lengths of her tangerine smelling skirt to rub all over the startled boy's face whilst she congratulated herself on what was, obviously, her superior teaching methods.

William coughed more. The tangerine stench was getting up his nose. Miss Terrine continued to scour the boy's face so hard that he felt like he was one of his Mum's cooking pots being scrubbed to an inch of its life. "Get *off!*" but William's cries were muffled.

"There, there, dear boy, there, there."

Conniving Cat scowled at William. He just smirked back, and before he knew what he was doing he had stuck out his tongue as far as it would go. "Blimey, Belle, that *does* feel good."

Miss Terrine wrenched the black and white picture of the terracotta fruit bowl, consisting of a prickly pineapple surrounded by cherries, a plum and a strange escapee avocado, from William's waif-like grasp and strode back to the head table. William smiled, and peered down at the most miniscule elfin thing stamping its foot on his desk. Both feet. He peered closer and closer down at his accomplice, having to bend further and further onto his desk top to actually see him at all.

The tiny odd thing was now hiding himself in the ink well of William's old wooden desk. God, it was drowning in ink. He dragged it out and plopped it on his desk.

"Thanks, Wills." It shook blue ink everywhere.

"Aaaaaah, what? Mum's gonna kill me, this shirt is ruined." William tried to brush the blue ink from his clothes, but he just succeeded in staining his hands.

"How about a bit of thanks, for the artwork?"

"Oh, thanks," William whispered.

"That's okay, you're welcome. Can *you* now help *me?*" replied the elf, tipping his acorn-shaped cap in William's direction. Then William realised it was indeed a real acorn shell. "Now you really *do* have to help us," the elf continued in terror. "Anouka speaks of nothing but Wills and Rosabella when it comes to the need for saving its people. *FROM DEATH*." The elf cried and cried so hard he slipped off William's desk onto the floor, and scurried along to the front of the classroom to blow his nose on Miss Terrine's tangerine stinking skirt just as Miss Terrine started to rustle about in a basket full of old tissue paper. The elfin thing, gripped to her tails, flew up into the air as the woman's skirt swished everywhere. William tried to follow the palaver taking place in Miss Terrine's clothing and at one point the elfin thing disappeared altogether only to reappear out of the top of her starched collar. She scratched her wrinkled neck.

"Damn wasps!" Miss Terrine flapped her arms about and knocked the elfin clean away.

William gasped. "Oy, come back," he stammered in a very audible whisper as he saw the acorn shell fly across the room and land in Conniving Cat's pencil case. She snapped it shut.

"Cheat!" Conniving Cat trapped the elf.

"Get lost!" William hated that girl, but the elfin managed to squeeze himself out through a hole in her pencil case and returned, trying to make his way back to William's ink well for safety. He scratched his way back up William's leg before landing again in the sticky blue stuff. Blue ink stained William all the way up to his knee, and then past that onto his upper leg. "*Ouch*, get off…" William pinched his thumb and finger together and picked the elf off his bare-skinned thigh and plonked him back in place with a thud.

"Careful!" the elf demanded. "Dropping me from that height could break my bones. It's like you being dropped from the roof of your house!"

"Oh, sorry. Who *are* you?"

The elf did not reply. He rubbed his bruised bottom, frowning and looked quite annoyed.

"Does it?" William changed the subject "Anouka, does it really only speak of Belle and I?" He looked surprised, but felt pathetically heroic inside. "Did Naribu send you?"

"Naribu? No. I came by myself." The elf looked about, cautiously. Miss Terrine was singing away to herself and plastering William's still life drawing on the wall for best possible exposure. "Naribu is but only our guide. He is old nowadays. Quite frail."

"Oh."

"He needs a mind like yourselves, yours and your sister's, to rid our world of the…" William could tell this innocent little elf could barely bring himself to mention her name and the tiny little thing just crumbled again, wailing so loudly that William was sure Miss Terrine would hear. "…the B-B-B-Black Witch," the elf stammered and his face turned pure white at just the mention of her name. "I can't stay long. The Black Witch has an accomplice already here, already roaming free in this world to soon let *her* in. The accomplice could be…here."

William looked at Conniving Cat. She seemed to be painting, frantically, mauve and lilac and black oil paints flicking everywhere. It was so obvious she was trying to get her painting on Miss Terrine's sudden wall of fame. But really, lilac lemons? Was Conniving Cat for real?

"He is surely in disguise…and listening?" The elf blinked back tears, ponderously, and regarded the classroom as if all he could think of was some anomaly hiding somewhere.

"How do you know it's a *he*?"

"I don't. Just saying," the elf went on. "Once this servant befriends four children, and persuades them to encircle the old oak tree, then the portal will open as *wide* as the dark side of Anouka itself," the elfin opened his arms until they could reach out horizontally no further. "…and all the evil it possesses, it will escape, and your school, it will be no longer. It will be her castle," the elf whimpered, looking cautiously around, and keeping his ear to the desk. "I must go. I can't be seen here." Tears gushed and he slipped over in his own puddles of salty water as he made his escape.

"What's your name? I didn't catch your *name!*" William cried as the elf ran off through the open sash window leading to the grumbling oak tree. "What are you called?"

"We should call it, *Can't Believe it Happened Fruit Heaven*," Miss Terrine announced.

"What?" William looked at the bony-cheeked art teacher.

"Your picture, William, we shall call it, *Can't Believe it Happened Fruit Heaven*. That's decided, then."

"Whatever." William did not care.

"They call me Myriad." And the elf disappeared.

"William, curb your tongue?" Miss Terrine interrupted the bell as it rang for the end of the lesson. "Quietly, please, boy. I know *you* quickly finished your drawing, but please, others are still working, child."

"Whatever, Miss," William mumbled, trying to get out the classroom and find Belle and Angus. His feet could not help but fidget and jiggle under his table top in anticipation to leave. "Well? Can we go?"

Miss Terrine ignored the question.

"Well? It's 12:02pm now?"

Miss Terrine carried on sipping her enormous cold mug of coffee.

"*WELL?*"

"Dismissed," Miss Terrine finally admitted.

"'bout time." And William, quite out of the ordinary and totally out of character, was the first to gather up his belongings and be outside in the fresh air.

"Changed, quite changed, that William Joy," Miss Terrine uttered, looking completely bemused. "What a sudden pace about him this Autumn term. At last."

"Belle, Belle! Angus!" William shouted and raced across the concrete tennis court. "Wait up." His cry had quietened to more of a whisper. *Wait up.* He realised he did not want to draw attention to himself. They had no idea who or what could be listening close by. To William, every child and every teacher looked suspicious. How on earth could he even begin to fathom out the goblin's disguise?

Belle stopped in her tracks and turned to face her brother, squinting. Angus missed the ball that she had thrown completely in the wrong direction. "Belle, that was a terrible try! Up your game, if you want to win!" cried Angus, launching himself towards a tennis ball they were indeed practicing to catch for winter sports day. Winter sports day was an entirely new concept, and no other school in the area offered such a thing.

"Winter sports day? Whatever next?" Miss Lovett had said rather loudly in assembly that morning as the new initiative had been announced.

"Not entirely sure that it's relevant or indeed at all necessary, and it certainly does not fit the school curriculum this year," Miss Terrine had followed up nodding and tutting alongside most of the other traditional teachers.

"'*Strange but true*' goes the saying." Mr Hardy had broken into the conversation. "We have to move with the times and get these children fit and ready."

"Ready for what?" Miss Terrine had replied with a hint of sarcasm in her voice. "A good dose of art is *much* better for the soul." And the old-fashioned arts teacher had clicked her heels and headed off to prepare her vivid water colours. "Winter sports day, they'll all be off sick for a week after that."

"Exactly," Miss Lovett had continued. "The children play enough sport to keep the tennis association buoyant for years to come. Do we *really* need another sports day, and a day that will most likely be cold and miserable, but I guess I can't change Professor Vixonight's newest request." And Miss Lovett had pottered off to attend to her English poetry tales for that afternoon muttering

"New headmasters and their offhand bright ideas, goodness me, the children will be huddling together for warmth out there, goodness me."

"Listen up." William pulled his dishevelled-haired sister and Angus together; their heads colliding as he dragged them to the floor, shaking.

"Careful, William, Mum's right, stop being so brutal, *and* your shoes are scuffed, again." Belle picked at her brother's fraying leather uppers.

"Oh *Shut Up*, Rosabella!" William tugged her messy plait until she was practically on the floor.

"OUCH! Bully!"

"Alyssa's right. A Black Witch *is* heading for our school. She can get through a portal in the old oak tree as *wiiiiiiiide* as Anouka itself if we don't prevent it happening. Myriad told me." William rattled off his morning, and wiped a few beads of perspiration from his brow. The afternoon sun was boiling.

"Myriad, what's that?" Belle and Angus asked in unison, sweating under the sun's burning rays. "Can we trust it?"

"It's not an '*it*', it's a '*him*', and well..." William thought, and looked at the blackened oak tree. It in turn grumbled back and then a branch whipped its ugly, dry leaved twigs at the boy's head; he ducked just in time. "We have no choice…RUUUUUN!" William shouted, and before the lively deep set tree could take a second swipe at the unsuspecting trio they had all ducked and grovelled their way to the school gate, knees scraped and clothing ripped in the worst place for any Mother to be able to darn. "My skin, it's hanging off!"

"Don't be so dramatic," Belle cried back. "It's my hair that's being dragged into the soil. Ouch!"

"You should brush it more often then."

"That's got nothing to do with it! This earth is alive," and Belle swore she saw little wrinkled fingers try to pull her further down.

The ground beneath the children gave way to each of their limbs as they tried to scramble free, but one by one the compounded soil swallowed them up.

"William, Belle!" each dizzy twisting child heard Alyssa cry out. "Angus! Just don't look her in the eye. DON'T LOOK HER IN THE EYE! DON'T HOLD THE BLACK WITCH'S STARE! I did…with *awful* consequences." Then. Darkness.

"Myriad?" William whispered. "Is that you?"

Inside Krook

"William?" whimpered a little tired voice. "Go back, *please* go back. It's not safe here, and if you're here, you're not back there, and back there is where we really need you."

"I can't, I can't, and I shan't, I really shan't. Where *are* you? You keep moving, Myriad." William cast his large enquiring eyes about inside the vast darkness that lay before him. "Myriad? What is that vile smell?" Immediately, the three dirty, soiled children pinched their noses whence the most horrific lurid pungent odour filled the air around them.

"William, it's the Black Witch's lair. I'm trapped in it. She has the most terrible creatures guarding her chambers. *Please* go back, I demand you to head...", but Myriad's voice trailed off as a deep cackle approached and eleven large black indecently sized hairy limbs hovered in mid-air above the children's scalps.

"JESUS!" Belle screamed. "Run!" She flapped her arms frantically about her face and in the air directly above her; wiry hair and hot breath touched her palms. "Oh GOD, this is horrendous! I hate it!" Just as one thick hairy leg brushed Belle's cheek, a small distant light depicted a way forwards, or was it backwards? She had no idea. Her eyes were panicking and her mind was nowhere good. She had fallen a great distance inside the old oak tree's trunk and after plenty of twisting and tumbling in the dark, Alyssa's voice getting fainter as she fell deeper, no one knew which way was out or indeed further in. The spider's rough legged bristles now scraped Belle's neck. A gaping hole opened up in her throat, and blood poured down her skin.

"BELLE!" Angus pulled the girl to the floor. She felt rigid. Her flashing eyes just stared forwards. "Belle?" Angus shook the ashen girl but she did not move, or reply.

"William, Belle's been petrified!" Angus cried. "She is totally hypnotised and out cold. She won't say a thing, and her eyes? They're just staring blankly ahead, at nothing."

"Sh...Sh...She's been poisoned," Myriad piped out breathlessly from somewhere. William and Angus looked directly up. Right above their heads, hanging from a thickly woven dark silver saliva covered spider's web, Myriad was stuck fast.

"Myriad, oh *Myriad*. How did you get *there*? Who put you in that disgusting web?" William whispered, trying not to attract any more attention. Angus battled next to him, trying to fight off the ever-closing-in spiders, they were approaching in clusters and William could not distinguish the end of one from the beginning of the next. How could he escape without actually touching their fangs?

"This is a pretty scary predicament, but hey, I've seen worse, in Arbrooth. You should have seen my pet's cage one Easter. Not a fluffy bunny in sight, but two fiery rats seemed to be always getting out. Much like most of the town, I guess." Angus pretended to duck and dive, still cradling Belle in his arms.

"Angus, Belle's out cold, you can't charm her now with all this heroic stuff. Get a grip! Idiot." William slunk as close to the floor as he could. His mouth scraped across some really sharp stones, and he felt his lips start to cut open. "What shall we *do*, Myriad? How can we release you? Any brave idea, Angus?"

"Don't ask me, I'm just bravado, and when I woke up this morning, I didn't expect to be down here this afternoon." Angus slapped Belle's cheeks. Both of them. "Nope, she's deffo out of it."

"You're such an idiot. Who brought you along, anyway?" William hid within the shadows cast by the spiders. They were now really deep inside the old oak tree's chambers. "*Blimey*, you're swinging right back into the most gigantic spider's path, Myriad!" and William leapt up high trying to reach for the elf's legs to wrench him down. He had to breathe in to avoid the black deathly limbs.

"It's no good, William," Myriad cried down. "The Black Witch has too many evil traps and blood thirsty servants. I tried to creep back into Anouka, through into the light side, but my movements were noticed, this tree has eyes everywhere. Krook captured me. Krook's spiders have vindictive spines. One has brushed Belle and p-p-p-poisoned her...outright," Myriad sobbed. There was no stopping his massive tears. "The old oak tree only has an opening into Krook, the dark side. The light side is not far, but I didn't quite make it back." Myriad sobbed so hard, his floods of tears made a river torrent on the path beneath William's feet.

"What or *who* is Krook?" William panted, reaching higher to grasp the elf's long pointed toes. It was no good, Myriad was too high up.

"Krook..." Myriad lowered his tone. "Krook, oh Krook..." Myriad sobbed, and William tried to understand the elf's words through his bawling mouth.

"Krook...it's the real name for the dark side of Anouka. We hardly dare say the name outside of its domain for fear of raising her, her, her...the Black Witch."

"Nice!" Angus muttered.

"Angus!" William thrashed out at him. "S-H-U-T U-P!"

"How can we save Belle, then?" Angus stroked her hair.

"Oh God, not another fly-by-night crush," William groaned.

"Shut up, yourself!" Angus argued back. "I was just getting dirt out of her hair."

"*This* is no time for *that!*" Myriad pointed to his feet which were practically inside one of the spider's mouths.

"They're a bit iffy, erratic?" William shouted up.

"The spiders? They're blind," Myriad cried down. "We need to destroy the one who petrified her." The closest spider sniffed its giant black nose in their direction. "To save Belle we need to destroy...*that!*" and Myriad, struggling but stuck entirely entwined in the spider's sticky web, faltered and gasped in fear pointing to the spider homing dauntingly in.

"Take *that!*" a high pitched scream fell from the light crack in the distance which Belle had noticed before her petrification, and a tall girl tumbled inside. "You miserable beast! D-I-E!"

"*Alyssa!*" William cried.

"I couldn't leave you down here, alone." Alyssa smashed the unprepared spider in the guts. "I had no intention of coming back, I *really* didn't," she cried whilst she stabbed and stabbed into the air, "...but I just couldn't leave you all down here, to die."

"Oooooooooooooh!" Angus blew kisses their way.

"SHUT UP!" William and Alyssa stared at the Scottish reprobate.

"The Black Witch, she is fearsome and deathly beyond belief. If you think her servants and accomplices are horrible, they are *nothing* compared to her." And Alyssa plunged her emerald jewelled sword further and deeper into the lead spider's grotesque muscular torso. Green liquid oozed out everywhere and dripped onto the floor, mixing in with Myriad's rushing river of tears. "Don't let it touch you. Get out of its way!" Alyssa hit her sword onto the crumbling wall. "Climb up here, get up the wall, don't let the green stuff touch you!"

Alyssa clung to a rock which stuck out from where she had fallen in, and William and Angus heaved Belle onto a dodgy misshapen ledge made up of roots and stinking fungus.

"What *is* that?" Angus peered, eagerly and closely, at the device now plunged entirely into the giant insect. It was covered in thick green blood. Only its golden handle stuck out, glinting.

"This? Oh, I stole it from Krook when I fell in here last summer." Alyssa shook her golden hair from side to side. It swayed. Ridiculously.

"Are you for real?" Angus uttered back.

"I never got to see the light side of Anouka; its streams and its mountain springs and its haven of animals and birds, I hear. But I am determined to destroy the Black Witch now before she enslaves us all," Alyssa hissed, and wrenched the emerald sword from deep within the spider, whose body immediately deflated with a grotesque stench, steam filling the cave. Its eleven legs caught fire. Then it shrivelled up until it was gone. The river evaporated until there was nothing left but a drop caught in a pothole.

"I heard Myriad's tale." Alyssa continued to shake out her rich, resplendent hair until it could not catch William's attention any more before he was completely hypnotised in her beauty, before she spoke out.

"I think I'm going to be sick," Angus silently acted out, sticking his fingers down his throat and gagging to the floor. William shot him an evil glare.

Angus stuck out his tongue.

"Humans, they're so ungainly." Myriad still hung there. "Hello, anyone going to cut me down?"

***

Alyssa herded everyone up the tunnel. The light got closer and closer and as it got brighter Belle's eyes began to focus. "Oh Angus!" She rushed to hug him.

"Is this some awful sickly lovesick Shakespeare play?" William pushed his way forwards. "Belle, you're not Hermia, you know, and Angus, there's no way you're going to be either of Lysander or Demetrius. And Myriad, do *not* play Puck."

"William, are you *quite* alright?" Myriad spat green splats from his mouth, and picked at his fingers.

"Oh Angus!" Belle continued to stare right at the boy.

"Now now, we only saved you. That's all." Angus trembled in Belle's grasp. She felt nice.

"Get off her," William prised her away.

"Just, listen. I have to tell you this," Alyssa whispered, then swung her sword randomly. It cut Myriad free with its piercing blade. Myriad fell from the dried out web and landed on William's head. "The Black Witch does not only seek four children to encircle this tree." Alyssa leant further in. "She seeks four certain souls." She glanced at the group and nodded.

"Four souls, as in dead ones?" William added.

"Of course, idiot," Angus muttered back.

"Really?" Belle tried to get back on track, she squeezed Angus's hand. William did not look amused.

"You mean *us*, don't you?" Angus shook. "*Why* did my parents move from Arbrooth? Poor decision, Mama. The cat fights next door were so not an issue." Angus scuffed his feet.

"When we encircle this tree from the outside, the soaring heat will be in demise and only the coldness of Krook will remain," Alyssa continued in a light whisper. "The Black Witch entrusted me last summer. She thought she had entranced me and told me to gather you together and bring you to her. I did not hold her gaze, it was just through a mirror on a crooked wall. The Black Witch thought she had me bewitched, she thought I was her slave, but I had tricked her quite by chance. On her wall, in her secret green chamber, four portraits lie."

"Of us, I suppose?" Angus moaned once again, quite bored of being stuck in the depths of a tree when he could be sunning himself outside. "I thought I was going to at least get a bit of a tan down South." He rolled his eyes.

"Idiot," William cursed.

"Will you *please* stop calling me that?"

"Yes, Angus. Yes, us four. You *do* complain. Who brought you?" Alyssa hissed back, but her words were slammed to the deck…"*DUCK!*" A slithering noise sounded all around and the most almighty snake hissed back at her, its yellow blanched forked tongue then turning to Angus forcing him to the floor. It seemed to hate him. Its smell was grotesque.

"Blimey…" Angus wailed, "….thanks, Alyssa!" he cried back at her, sarcastically. "Did *you* bring all these beasts? What's next? A repressed tiger?" Angus lay, his heart beating out of control, on the chamber's dusty dry floor vowing never to trust Alyssa ever again. But Alyssa? She had slayed the beast. Cut it in half with one slice.

"You're welcome, Angus Moon." Alyssa smiled, and tossed her hair in the most incredulous, most ridiculous way he had ever seen and knocked him to the floor once again just as he had gotten his balance. "Now. Where *was* I?"

"Stupid girls."

Alyssa pointed her nose ahead. "All our names were set out written in blood on the Black Witch's green chamber wall. We are her destiny, but we have to change that."

"Count *me* in," Angus sat bolt upright. "Count me in for sure. I don't want to see another accomplice or evil servant ever again, please." He felt quite out of breath. "And if it means I get one of those swords? Cool! And if it gets rid of you out of my life too, the better." He mumbled the last bit. Alyssa stamped on his foot as he tried to get up for the third time. "*Jeeeees.*"

"Me neither," Belle intervened. "Did I lose some time? Are you Myriad? You're safe. You're TINY."

"Alright, don't get me started on sizest rationale. Are you aware of *Chapter II, Section IX*, girl?"

"Uuuur, no," Belle shut up.

"Right then."

"Get with it, you guys." Alyssa strutted on. Angus was sure her hair was actually getting more voluminous as she walked. It was ridiculous.

"I know these chambers, and there really is no time to lose. Follow me." And the quick witted elf took a sudden dip down a very, very, very tight pathway.

"Shouldn't we be heading for that chink of light, from where Alyssa fell?" William butted in, pointing to the furthest, highest end of the tunnel walls. "That's the way out, isn't it?"

"It's guarded," Alyssa replied. She glanced around, her senses suspicious of everything. Her pupils were enormously black and she twitched at every shadow that flickered on the charcoal coloured wall. "You see, the Black Witch believes I am bringing you all to her. To fulfil her quest that Krook grows into the most powerful creation ever known. The Black Witch needs us all. We will sit at each compass point around this old oak tree and the world will be all powerful to her. She believes I am her accomplice and her guard let me through. I am to surrender you to her and we will all become betrothed under her influence, ever virtuous to her." Alyssa shivered. "Follow Myriad, quick, before we are noticed."

"Weirdo," Angus muttered.

"Alyssa?" Belle ran to catch her up. "Alyssa, what will the Black Witch do to you when she realises you've betrayed her?"

"Oh, let's not think about that."

"I can think of something," Angus answered for her.

"Now, shoot, down here," Alyssa ignored Angus and pushed everyone further into the tunnel. It was much narrower than before, and in places the roof above their heads was so low even Myriad, the smallest most nimble-footed individual, had to cower right down. "Faster, come on." Alyssa hurried through the tiniest of tunnels, some lined with really prickly thorns.

"Ouch, this is ridiculous!" Angus moaned once more. "Why are we trusting you anyway?"

"And where would you go now without her? Any other bright ideas? Back that way with the other deadly arachnids?" William walked on.

"Be quiet, we have to escape this way, either that or the Black Witch will sense we are here. Beware of what you say, even the walls have ears, heads down," Alyssa whispered.

Scraping their knees, and their palms completely covered in dirt, William, Belle and Angus continued to crawl behind Alyssa, the tunnel getting narrower and skinnier and dirtier until thick green roots with small amounts of moss began to poke through the dry dead brown leaves which had, up until now, been the only nature covering the floor.

"Life! Alyssa, you've guided us to Anouka's light side. I really don't think it has a name, just Anouka." William stared at his surroundings. "Naribu?" he stared into a distance which seemed miles and miles away. "Naribu? Is that you?" An owl seemed a tiny dot on the horizon.

Alyssa stood up tall. The tunnel had come out into the most endearing meadow where the crispy dead tree bark had been left far behind and only soft red and yellow autumnal leaves waved in the breeze. Young rosy apple trees sprung up all around. "Myriad, thank you. I have only ever dreamt of seeing the beauty Anouka holds. All I knew was the dark side," Alyssa would not mention its name.

Professor Vixonight

"Now *this* is more like it." Angus stuck out his chest and strolled around on the velvet green grass. He kicked off his black school shoes to allow the soft, nearly turquoise, shaded blades to wriggle between his toes. "Yep, glad we moved down from Arbrooth now. Sun and blue skies, which I've only ever seen in movies, right here."

"Fickle." Alyssa shook her head Angus's way.

"Arbrooth can't be *that* gloomy? You're just teasing us, aren't you?" Belle nudged her Scottish friend.

"Flirt." William cast Belle a deathly look.

"Aye, it wasn't *all* that bad, I guess," Angus put on his strongest accent which annoyed William even more. He breathed in the clean Anoukan air, reminiscing back to his old Scottish grey flint cottage built along a grey pea-shingle street under, generally, a very dark grey cloudy sky. "But I can't quite remember much good about it either. No colour like this."

"Myriad, how do we get home?" William turned to the elf.

"Home? Uuuuur? Well…" The elf looked mildly confused. "I didn't really take note of my surroundings when I found you in your art class, William."

"You mean we're stuck here?" Angus replied. "Cool! I certainly didn't fancy that maths test tomorrow. Professor Vixonight keeps looking at me as if I have two heads. Every time I even slightly glance out the window, he is on me like a preying hawk. He mocked the headmaster's tone. *"Angus Moon, what is out that window which is more interesting than fractions this morning, boy? Can you see someone, out there, out by that old oak tree? Well?"* Angus threw back his scruffy hair. "He's quite shady, don't you think, that new headmaster? I think so anyway." Angus casually kicked his way through the dewy meadow. The light was fading as the sun set low. "Have we got to stay all night? AWESOME, man! *A-w-e s-o-m-e!*"

"Mum shan't miss us, Anouka is timeless." Belle smiled, taking Angus by the hand.

Angus blushed.

"For Heaven's sake…" William squeezed between the two companions, "can't you just play it down, you know, just for us? Anyway, staying all night, I don't think that will be necessary, Angus. I am sure we can find our way home. Can't we?" William looked at Alyssa, sternly.

"Me?" Alyssa replied, candidly. "Me? I've never ever been to the light side." Alyssa looked around, envious she had only ever experienced the realm of the Black Witch. "It's just so beautiful here."

"Angus?" William suddenly shot the new boy a glance. "Blimey, Angus!"

"What is it?" Angus quickly span around full circle to make sure no abhorrent creatures were about to pounce on him. He had had enough of that game.

"I've just realised. Heaven's above, perhaps Professor Vixonight thinks *you* are, well, from Anouka?" William spoke out. "He's new to our school. Bit odd that our old headmistress just disappears and Professor Vixonight arrives; dark and scathing in appearance. I bet *he's* the goblin. I'm almost sure he has something dark about him. I'm certain. He probably thinks you're from the light side, come to depower the Black Witch. You are new around here," William tossed his arms about. "Who are you really, Angus Moon?"

Alyssa looked at Angus. "Is he onto something Angus? Is William onto something?" She nodded with a frown encrusted on her brow. "Who *are* you?"

"Perhaps Professor Vixonight is in fact the Black Witch herself?" Belle whispered their worst fear. "Already penetrating our world?"

"What, a man? A man dressed as a woman? In Hollingbourne? No, she hasn't escaped yet, has she?" Angus threw in his two pence worth and addressed Myriad who sat, biting his long yellow finger nails and looking quite helpless.

"Me? I have no idea. I suppose she could have easily got through to our world by now...perish the thought that her black magic and wisdom might allow her to trap us around that old oak tree. Perish the thought..." Myriad shook, his lips trembling at the mere idea.

"This is useless. We can't just stand here throwing around accusations. We have to stay vigilant. Trust no one. Seriously." William faced his friends. "The goblin could be one of us?" William peered at Angus, then to Alyssa in turn. "You're both new around here?"

"William, don't be absurd!" cried Belle. "You just told us to stop throwing around banal accusations. You actually *saw* Angus petrified of the goblin himself by the pond. He was wrecked at its appearance, before he even saw us. It wasn't for show, was it Angus?" Belle frowned at the Scottish boy and then turned her eyes to blondie. "And Alyssa, she submerged her sword into that dreadful spider. You can't possibly think it's any of us? You'll be saying *I'm* the Black Witch next!" Belle stomped off after Angus who had turned his back to get a sun tan.

"Nothing surprises me," William muttered. "You can be a witch sometimes, Rosabella."

"I heard that."

"William, you know me, Alyssa. We've been friends forever." The tall girl battered her eyes at William.

"I know. I'm sorry. It's just that everyone could be someone or something they're not showing. How am I supposed to know? You could be in disguise and the real Alyssa tied up in a tree. Wish that Angus actually was! If we don't stop Kroo..." William managed to zip his mouth and not finish his sentence. "...if we don't stop the dark side, our village, it's doomed."

"At least there'd be no school dinners, ever again!" Angus shouted back from his horizontal position on the floor. "Aaaah, this is the life."

"How did he hear that from right over there?" William frowned at Alyssa, but she did not reply.

"Doomed? Nonsense!" Alyssa put her arm on William's bent over shrugged shoulder. "Absolute nonsensical ridiculousness. We *will* stop her!" That was enough to make William snap out of creating such cumbersome ideas. "Come on, then. What are you waiting for?" Alyssa shook William by the shoulders, and he felt young and protected again like during his first years as a new boy in school. "You were new once, remember?" she remarked.

"Get a room," Angus replied.

***

The sun was now so low in the orange sky it was becoming increasingly difficult to see. Long large shadows of the four ambling figures crossed the deepening green meadow all around, and a slight breeze was picking up.

"It's quite chilly tonight, isn't it?" Belle pulled her royal blue cardigan further up around her neck, which was gradually producing goose bumps, and tried to move closer to Angus. Hinting.

"He doesn't need any encouragement, Rosabella," William muttered, sauntering behind.

Belle huddled even closer to Angus and William knew she did it to annoy him. But then he noticed something. Angus stood tall and rigid, seemingly not relinquishing any friendly warming cuddle in return.

"Maybe he's bored of you now, Rosabella."

"What's up? Why are you ignoring me, Angus?" Belle saw his eyes glance over towards her elder brother. That was a first. William just looked back and held Angus's gaze; but William suddenly did not presume anything this time and just nodded. He looked fazed. William shocked himself, and then he glared at Myriad. *Approval*, Angus depicted. "You cunning little so and so," William tutted at the elf.

"No idea what you're taking about." Myriad whistled.

"You're both weird." Belle shuffled even closer, looking at her brother and then at the Scot. "And don't worry about *him*." Belle whispered, pointing her head towards William. But Angus had already taken Belle's hand.

***

The last deep burnt orange segment of sunshine sank lower than the meadow's horizon itself, and the figures shivered. The lush green fields were now a torrid dark grey, and the flowers' bright yellow and red heads had closed up for the night. Darkness fell. Although there was still a sweet smell of fruit lingering.

"Hell, what was *that?*" Angus pricked up his ears and shrieked as the dark silver moon replaced the sun in the navy sky and lit up the ground. "What on earth was that rumble? That low, penetrating, lingering growl in fact. You did hear it, didn't you?" Angus clenched Belle's palm tighter than ever before.

"Hero? Pah," William tutted.

"I don't know. I have absolutely no idea," Belle looked about, hesitantly.

"I thought you said this was the light side, William?" Angus glanced around in a staccato fashion trying to figure out from exactly where the growl was coming.

"I did, and it is. Anouka can be lovely, but I can't monitor who or what comes in or out. If the Black Witch has escaped, perhaps she has come here first?" William tried to assemble some sort of reply but it did not alter the fact that something very nasty was very close by. The growl sounded again, much nearer this time. A huge black silhouette filled the air around them. It encircled its victims.

Angus's eyes darted about. "If you shout *R-U-N* one more time, Belle, I swear I'll…"

"*R-U-N* just *R-U-N*!" Belle cried.

"Where to?" Angus shouted back. "The shadow, it's everywhere. This gargantuan black shadow is right on us, but, but, I really can't see the perpetrator at all! Can you?" Angus threw out the question to anyone who was listening.

"No! Just an enormous dark beastly shadow with dripping fangs and a thick set tail! That's all I can see! Is that enough?" William cried.

Alyssa looked ahead. In the distance, the opposite side of the field to where the old oak tree stood, a faint chink of light shone brightly. "Over there! Look, follow me over there. I have no idea where that bright white opening leads but it's our only chance! Quick!" and Alyssa grabbed William's hand and dragged him full pelt across the damp meadow. The light grew larger and larger, and closer and closer, and the gnarling beast just followed, gritted teeth depicted in its shadow.

"What *is* that thing?" Angus panted as he raced right behind in Alyssa's tall striding footsteps. "It's like some sort of absolutely menacing enormous dog? Anyway, I'm not s-c-a-r-e-d…" Angus panted on, flicking his ruffled hair. "The cats were more menacing in Arbrooth..."

"Give it a rest!" William looked, and saw Angus's face was whiter than white. "You're such a liar! Anyway, I think it's a werewolf!" William whispered in Angus's ear.

"A *WHAT?* For the life of..."

Shooting a glance behind to where they had all just been standing, William tried to look back and run forward. The most massive of all moons appeared and then so did that thing. "I'm sure of it. It *is* a werewolf!" and William fell to the floor. "W-o-a-h! Where on earth *are* we?" Silence.

"It's someone's house? We're in someone's living room. Look, photos, a fireplace...even books, school books." William strolled over to take a closer look. "Maths books, ha ha Angus, all for you! *And* reports. Blimey, all these reports are from our school, look, here's Isla's, oh and Robyn's, oh and *yours* Belle."

"Give that here, oy, *give* that to me!" Belle tried to grab her school report before her brother opened it up to take a look inside.

"Trying to hide something?" William held the report way above his head out of his sister's grasping hands.

He stuck out his tongue in return to Belle's pointy one. "You *do* look annoyed, look at your face, it's so puffy! Got something you don't want me to know?" William danced about. "I'm sure it's perfect, Belle, you're such a teacher's pet." He passed the report to her. She just scowled back.

"Cretin."

"I just want to know whose house we have ended up inside. That werewolf practically drove us in. Don't you think?"

A sharp scratching noise battled at the door.

"Shall we let it in?" Angus puffed out his chest.

"Idiot!" William looked at Angus. "If that door wasn't there, I don't think you'd be showing such bravado."

Silence. The noise stopped. "It did rather feel that way. The werewolf driving us here." Angus backed up to the wall. "It did seem to chase us right inside in fact. Do you think it's a trap?"

"A trap indeed?" and the four trembling figures span around in turn as a deep, menacing, questioning but familiar voice entered the room from the darkest corner. A figure emerged. A figure which started to rise from the floor, to stand taller on two legs, and taller and taller still, and hairier.

"P-P-Professor Vixonight!" trembled Belle. "We, we just needed a place to hide. This is your house? Sorry, so sorry. We were being chased, by the most menacing werewo..." but she stopped in her tracks as William hit her arm.

"Sorry, Professor, uuuur, we'll just be leaving now." William walked backwards towards the door through which they had just fallen, and then tried to edge around the periphery of the wall to another, larger, wooden door. He had no intention of meeting that werewolf again. "Oh!" the boy jumped up, both feet leaving the floor. He had kicked over a chrome bowl full of river pond water and algae. It flooded the floor. Professor Vixonight did not appear to own a dog.

"Problem, boy?" Professor Vixonight peered closer as William appeared to move backwards without even shuffling his feet. Professor Vixonight moved nearer and peered closer still, fixated on William's bright blue wide eyes. The headmaster's eyes were now quite a deep glowing orange. Or was it the burning fireplace's reflective glare? He couldn't possibly be. It was not possible that *he* was the werewolf?

"No, no problem, we just fell into your rustic house by mistake. On our way home, come on." William beckoned his friends to follow. "See you tomorrow, Professor." The companions opened the second larger newest looking varnished door, as opposed to the wood worm eaten one in which they had entered the room.

"That was random!" Angus moaned as his steps quickened up the road. "Oh, we're opposite the pond. Well, glad I got us out of that scrape."

William shook his head. "I *knew* he was involved, I just *knew*. He has to be...the Black Witch, or another untrustworthy accomplice, or the goblin," William muttered as he tripped and stumbled along in the darkness of the night. It had become quite late since the end of school, and even the sun in the village had vanished.

"Why didn't he just, you know..." Belle's eyes were quite dry as she tried to bat back her tears, "...just maul us there, right there. He had us."

"Did you see that aged old fireplace?" Alyssa turned back as she spoke. She waded through what now seemed to be extremely dewy grass surrounding the pond. "Gross, that goblin threw all this rancid water out when he flung himself from the pond. It's gross." Sticky weeds got entangled in her feet.

"Yes, roaring, wasn't it?" William replied, in thought. "It should have made the room really hot, but I couldn't feel any heat. I was too busy trying to keep Vixonight at bay."

"I think you'll find *you* were backing away," Angus muttered.

"Backing away to find the only escape route. I didn't see *you* helping. Wimp."

"No, it was cold, dead cold, and just full of charcoal and old wood. It wasn't burning at all. Where were *you* looking?" Alyssa stared at William. "The fireplace was enormous, granted, but did you see the hair, the malted hair in the grate? All wiry and thick, black as soot it was, handfuls of it, just floating about. Animal hair, it really looked like......" Alyssa shuddered. "...werewolf hair?"

And that confirmed William's fears. Professor Vixonight's eyes were not at all reflecting orange flames from the inglenook, but they were in fact deep set orange in colour themselves. "He's the werewolf! Blimey, our headmaster is a werewolf." William spoke low, and looked at the moon.

The Lunchtime Forest

As thick as thieves the four companions sat, rigid, the following day. School dinner. Vile. This term there had been nothing more than mutton pie and ridiculous tropical fruit; musty fruit, and Professor Vixonight had been seen to sniff about, quite with the jitters, as soon as lunch was served. At the mere chink of sunlight in his classroom, the blinds would be drawn.

William, Belle, Alyssa, and, William thought, perhaps Angus Moon, had not been able to sleep or think of anything but that night. "Do you *really* think so?" Angus looked around the dinner hall. It echoed, always echoed. He spoke lower. "Do you *really* think the Professor is a werewolf?" Angus whispered so low, and bent so far across the table to William and Alyssa that the faces at the next table started to get suspicious.

"What are you whispering about?" Conniving Cat scorned. "Well? Cheating again, William?"

William and Alyssa both sat with their hands in their laps and their faces staring at their plates. Both were trying hard not to draw any further attention to themselves. Maths lesson that morning had been sickening. Professor Vixonight would not keep more than an arm's length from Angus's desk, and every move William made, the head teacher had pursued him as if he were prey.

"There can be no other explanation, Angus," William replied directly to his empty plate. He did not look up. "Bright orange fuelled eyes, coarse black hair sitting in clumps in the inglenook grate, bowls of stagnant water on the floor, and absolutely no sign of a pet. He *must* be a werewolf, *that* werewolf."

"Any werewolf, I'm not going to distinguish one from another. And I certainly hope there aren't any more. Not that I'm scared or anything…you should have seen the pets we had in Arbrooth…"

"Really, Angus? Listen to yourself," Alyssa raised both her hands.

"But why did he not capture us then and tear us to shreds?" Angus did not mince his words.

"Don't you understand?" Alyssa butted back in. She needs us. The Black Witch needs us to surround the old oak tree. All of us. For the Black Witch to prosper, we must be alive.

Belle coughed. "That is just gross," she replied. Conniving Cat leant closer. Belle opened her mouth in purposeful earshot of Cat. "What *are* we to do? We've

88

won the *Best Art of the Year Pupils*, again? Oh, we're just too good for that competition really, we should let someone else win one year, really we should. And you didn't have to put any effort in this time, William, you could have drawn that *Can't Believe it Happened Fruit Heaven* with your eyes shut. You'll win the County Art Show for sure in the Spring." Belle snubbed her nose in Conniving Cat's direction.

"Urrrr, I did," William replied. "I actually *did* do it with my eyes shut. I blinked and it was just there, no effort, the picture just…"

"Yes, yes, we all know that." Belle glared at her brother.

"Cheat," was all Conniving Cat could say.

"Snoop," Belle retorted.

"Belle, just leave her, she doesn't know anything." William twisted his back to Conniving Cat.

"You're still a cheat! I'll prove it one day." Cat took a bite of her tangerine. "V-I-L-E!" she spat it out.

"Hope you choke on it," Belle muttered.

"Problem, ladies?" Miss Terrine suddenly appeared by Belle's side, slyly regarding the girl over the tops of her spectacles. "If you have finished your lunch, kindly make room for others. Look, poor Isla has no seat."

"Oh, but there are plenty of seats always for everyone." Belle looked around. "How odd." She stood up. But it was true. There were far less wooden tables today, and a queue of pupils waiting to sit down. "Where are all the seats?"

Belle heard Isla whisper to Robyn. "Not mutton again, and look, this looks like Chinese stuff, not at all sure what the meat is though. Looks awful. Looks like chicken's feet." She retched so hard Belle thought she was actually going to be sick inside the entire vat. Not that it would have made much difference to the look, or the taste. Isla skipped that course and took a second helping of apple sauce, but even that looked brown and oldish, with a skin wrinkled on top. "Not entirely appetising," Isla complained and searched for a seat. "Might change to packed lunch next half term, at least it might not resemble dog food."

It was true. As Belle looked around the school dining room, and Isla searched for a seat on which to sit and just look at her sour apple sauce, it was no fallacy that there were indeed far less tables and even fewer chairs than even yesterday.

"Chop chop, ship shape, girls." Miss Terrine clapped her hands and hurried any pupil along that had less than half a bowlful of, what was supposed to resemble, dessert. "Belle, Alyssa, I can see your plates are practically clear. Make room for Isla and Robyn." And the two inseparable friends slipped in at the table as Belle and Alyssa stood up.

"Thanks," smiled Isla in Belle's direction as she spooned rather a large dollop of apple, pureed to a pulp, into her mouth. She immediately spat it out. "That is grotesque, don't try the fruit, Robyn, it has most definitely turned."

Belle frowned. So it was not just her palate. Everyone was feeling the desperate vile offerings that school dinners seemed to resemble lately. She looked around whilst she hovered behind her brother and Angus. Luckily, both boys had chosen salad and, despite the limp lettuce leaves which had seen better days and wrinkly tomatoes still covered in earth, the fish looked mildly promising. William and Angus were eating it in any event.

"Still *here*, Belle?" a deep gravelly voice suddenly spoke into her ear from behind. "Didn't Miss Terrine ask you to move on? You don't fancy outside today, tennis or drawing in the woods? A touch of magic to your nature poem might be found round that beast of an old oak tree, might it not?" the Professor proposed this to Belle, only, and then leant in towards Alyssa to offer similar thoughts Belle could only assume. Alyssa tried to look nonchalant.

Conniving Cat peered their way. "They're such cheats, sucking up to Vixonight. They'll come unstuck one day for sure. And when they do, I'll be there to watch them squirm."

"Uuuur, not today, thanks anyway." Belle backed away trying not to hold any sort of weird werewolfy stare with the man. If he could be called a man. "We're planning on sprinting practice right in the open up the field there," she lied. Professor Vixonight knew.

"Are you, are you indeed?" The hairy man breathed out a disgustingly rotten stench. Belle caught the worst of it. He held her gaze, and she blinked as much as she could to not be drawn right in.

"The field, the one right in view of everyone, that's where we'll be." Belle backed up further until her legs were practically out the door. She tumbled backwards, and pointed to the furthest part of the playground. "Making the most of the autumnal sun, especially hot for this time of year," Belle continued, a bead of perspiration from fear rather than heat slipping from her brow as she tried to steer away from his foul, drooling mouth. "Come on, Alyssa." And, as the girls quickened their steps and left the hall behind, Belle glanced back. "Blimey, William was right, Professor Vixonight's eyes *were* shining a deep set orange." He watched them leave. "You must be that werewolf," Belle whispered, quietly. But her undertone was loud enough for the headmaster's heightened senses to hear. His lips parted to reveal four long yellowing fangs. "Professor Vixonight!" and Belle ran as fast as she could. She dragged Alyssa behind.

"What *has* got into you, Belle?" Alyssa fell to the floor, breathless, when she finally stopped being dragged. She collapsed behind an enormous wooden den built by the little ones. "Why did you tear away like that?"

"Me?" Belle replied, trying to catch her breath. "Surely Professor Vixonight told *you* to go and hang out round the old oak tree too, no? Trying to get us all there to finish the Black Witch's work. He's trapping us one by one." Belle stood up to search for the boys. "Surely they shan't fall for Professor Vixonight's plan?"

"No, the Professor told me to make sure this massive wood crafted den here was safc, actually," Alyssa replied. "I'm head girl and he thinks I've been neglecting my duties. He told me that all these Anoukan things have completely taken over."

"Blimey."

"I know."

"He knows."

"Alyssa, you're not giving in, are you? Leaving us to fight the Professor and the Black Witch without you? *Alyssa!*"

"No, no of course not!" Alyssa whispered, harshly, lying on the floor. Bits of sticks and sharp stones were sticking into her thighs. "Give up? Why would you think that? I'm not fancying dying just yet. We just need to be careful, lie low for a while. If we act suspiciously around Vixonight, or anyone, it will reveal we know more than we should."

"What, so you're going to pretend to do stuff for him? He's going to catch you out, I know he will."

"Nope, he's a bloke. He's not going to catch anyone out."

"A *bloke?* Alyssa, he's not a bloke, he's a bleeding werewo…"

"Ssssssssss…" Alyssa lay there. She flicked her hair.

"And get *that* out my face." Belle swiped at the ridiculously long blonde hair. She did not like to be kept in the dark. "I suppose so." Belle looked at the floor, grumpily. "I suppose we could lie low. But Vixonight already knows we suspect him. Alyssa, for goodness sake, he just bared his fangs right at me, as we left the hall after lunch. He absolutely knows we know he's that werewolf."

"Let's see what William says."

"Thought you'd say that."

"Stop arguing," William threw himself down between Alyssa and Belle. Nearer to Alyssa, Belle realised. "Vixonight, he's getting to you, isn't he? That's his plan. He's one step ahead."

"No he's not, I *am* going to catch him out," Alyssa huffed back. "Belle, just be vigilant around Vixonight."

"You don't need to tell me what to do."

"See, he's doing it again. Making you argue, don't you get it yet?" William's voice was low and annoyed, and Alyssa turned to him.

"Did you see us come out here?"

"Yep. Anyway, see what I say about what?"

"Professor Vixonight, he bared his fangs at Belle and he asked her to sit around that old oak tree. I think we should just keep tight with our suspicions, not be heroic."

"Copy cat." Belle muttered.

"We neither possess black magic powers nor unnatural strength like the Black Witch and the werewolf. So for us, we need to play them, timing, strategy." Alyssa looked deadly serious.

"I can see why you're head girl, Alyssa." Angus moved closer. "Smart!" And then, to Belle's outrage, Angus winked at Alyssa.

Belle sat up. "Look, Alyssa, this den is made up of wood from the dining hall furniture. Had you noticed *that?* The oldest oak was used to make the tables and chairs centuries ago, when the school first opened..."

"Oh..."

".....*and*," Belle did not let Alyssa spoil her moment. "......*and* I remember reading in the library that the dining room furniture was so incredibly old it was sculptured from the school's own ancient forest. *That* old oak tree." She pointed its way.

Angus moved closer to Belle now. "How intriguing. Tell me more."

"Perhaps this is a trap?" Belle continued. "We have all been tricked by the Professor. This steadfast den is in fact part of the old oak tree."

"Full on, Belle, w-i-c-k-e-d," Angus was now so close to Belle's face it was sickening.

"Fickle," Alyssa mumbled.

"Jealous," Belle mumbled back

"He's done it *again*, catching you off-guard! Are all of you just *stupid*?" William stood up. "BLIMEY *R-U-N!*" and William, his heart in his mouth, paced as fast as he could further and further into the forest to where a leafy patch assumed a sudden great open space. He turned back. "Come on, then…idiots! Your arguing has gone to your heads."

"Well, well, well if I'm not mistaken, I *am* familiar with this vast open patch of greenery," Myriad's voice sounded as his pointed nose appeared from behind a red spotted toadstool stuck to William's trousers. "We are indeed towering above your school's entrance into the light side of Anouka, I am sure we are. Well, well, well…" the cautious elf spoke softly through his cupped hands.

"Where *are* you?" William shot his head about, but still tried to keep low.

"Here, right here!"

"Where's *here?*"

"*Here*, you're looking at me!"

"Myriad, this is no time for sill..."

"Myriad, you're *safe!* Oh *Myriad…*" Belle threw her arms around the gangling elf, knocking William to the floor.

"Watch out, idiot…" William rubbed his throbbing buttocks.

"Where did you get to after our visit to Vixonight's house last night?" Belle chatted to William's groin.

"Stop staring down there." William was starting to feel uncomfortable.

"Well, right here of course; in your brother's pocket. I thought he never cleans them out so I'll be safe…and safe I was. I knew I wasn't going to get thrown away."

Belle cackled. "That'd be right! Daylight has never even seen the insides of those trousers, but on the other hand, are you sure you didn't get poisoned by the unsavoury smell?" She held her nose and hopped about.

"Ssh, remember everywhere could lead to somewhere unsavoury, Belle." Myriad whispered. "Don't tell too much out loud."

"Aye, we don't all want to hear about the insides of William's trousers." Angus slithered along the floor.

"Anyway, where *are* we then?" She didn't laugh at Angus's joke. She still hadn't quite forgiven Angus for his flirting, flirting with Alyssa of all people. She glanced around. She had played in the forest loads of times but never had she gone so far inside. "These toadstools, they're enormous!"

"*Awesome*, don't you mean?" Angus dug Belle in the ribs but she completely ignored him, and instead she hopped up to sit high on the largest toadstool before Myriad had a chance to warn her.

"N-O-O-O-O-O-O-! Not *that* one, Belle, we must exercise caution, carefully choose which toadstool to...." but before Myriad could even grasp her hand the toadstool had grown quickly downwards, and disappeared; the earthy dust covering both it and Belle as if they had never been there at all.

"Belle, *B-E-L-L-E* come back!" William started digging at the empty dry earth beneath his feet. He scrabbled at the earth's hard surface, getting more dirt in his pockets and beneath his fingernails than digging any deeper. "Belle, oh Belle? Stick out your tongue, snub your nose at me, anything, I don't care about anything anymore, *BEEEEEEEELLE!*" William just stared at the solid ground. There was no way in. It was silent.

"Woah, dude! You *do* love your sister." Angus looked at the empty earth. It was an earth that had no Belle anymore. "Aye, she'll be back, when there's chocolate."

William still just stared at the floor. He put his hands into his pockets. Inside, right at the very bottom of the messiest one, he found a wrapper. It was quite old, but wrapped carefully, for a rainy day, he found some squares of sweet white stuff.

"........chocolate," Angus shouted. "Come on Belle, dig yourself out, William's sharing his chocolate, and I'm telling you, you'll never get an offer like that again. *Belle?*" Silence.

The sun got hotter and hotter and William still just stood there with the white chocolate melting between his fingers. He carried on picking at the ground, faster and faster, and then he heard a faint rumbling further into the woods. As he squinted in through the fiercely impenetrable thicket, a misty light seethed its way towards him and the trees themselves began to move. Not only did branches sway in the sudden breeze, a breeze which got heavier and heavier and branches which swiped nastier and nastier, but the entire forest of Printellicha bushes, Ferecklian hedgerows and Ardouscious firs wrenched themselves from the soil and dragged their rooted bodies towards him.

"Oh, yes." Myriad now nodded. "Yes, I remember this place now," and the elf scratched his messy haired scalp. "Yes, yes, it's coming back to me, indeed it is, now what happened the last time these trees became alive, let me think, it's all rather a blur…" Myriad scratched his scalp further until his crusty fingernails actually made it bleed. "I remember…*run for your lives!*" and Myriad took to his pointed heels, grabbing a jewelled wand from his belt, and disappeared into the greying thicket.

William just stared at the animate trees, and then to the floor where Belle was buried.

"Run now, didn't you hear me?" was all William could decipher from the lost elf's hair-raising cries. "Save yourselves. I was here once before, and the B-B-Black Witch nearly caught my gaze. Look down, don't stare at the trees, the trees they will bewitch you and you will be in her trance. Forever. I have seen others disappear right here, please be cautious! Follow me, or simply go back!" Myriad's voice was so faint now.

William realised there was no back. The trees were surrounding him closer and closer.

"I don't remember the way back, and the trees are all in our path and *where's my sister?*" William cried. "Myriad, help us here, please?" As the trees closed further in, crushing everything in their path leaving little to surrender, William curled into a ball on the floor. "M-y-r-i-a-d!"

As William cried Myriad's name as loud as he could an enormous spark filled the sky and showered ice white fire down onto the forest below. William covered his eyes for protection. The bright white light was sure to blind him. A voice called from a distance. "Follow the path, follow my path depicted in the shards of charcoal. Follow it," Myriad called. William grabbed Alyssa's frock and Angus's pullover sleeves and dragged them both along the burnt silver pathway.

"Hero?" William laughed in Angus's face. "Myriad, I thought you recalled this to be the entrance to the *light* side of Anouka? How can this be? It doesn't seem pleasant to me at all, not at all," cried William.

"Oh, you should have seen the thunderstorms of Arbrooth, this is summer camp compared to that…"

"...I sussed out *your* true colours ages ago, Angus."
William tripped over the burning shards.

"I can't dictate who guards every entrance." William smacked his leg as he heard Myriad whisper onto his thighs. "Oy! Careful!" Myriad was now back inside William's trousers. "Nice chocolate."

"Myriad, I thought you were a branch swiping at me, you've got to be careful yourself!"

"...but let's hope Belle found a nice way in. Some openings lead to the light and some to the dark side. Who knows until it could be too late?"

"Myriad, that's not really helping William. He fears for Belle. How can we get to her?" Alyssa looked around. All she could see were trees, trees dying everywhere. Branches were sizzling with the charcoaled remains of the flames. The grass was a crumbling pile of dust for miles around. The sky had completely disappeared.

Myriad looked at his emerald wand. It glinted in the decreasing sunlight. He sighed a terribly deep sigh. "Well, we could try *this*?" He looked, fearfully, at the rather cumbersome wand in his hand. "It did just grant a path to safety destroying evil trees, but it has got a life of its own. You can't trust it. You just have to hope for the best."

"Bit like Angus's contribution then," Alyssa sniggered. "Go on. Give it a try. We've nothing to lose…*except our heads if you don't hurry up.*"

It looked like the trees were starting to writhe on the floor, starting to get back some life. The swishing branches were actually scratching their dry barked trunks as if they were actually alive.

"Use it, just use it won't you? If you won't, *I* will!" Angus grabbed the wand from Myriad before anyone could stop him. "Aye wand, just do whatever you know. Those trees are regenerating themselves again. Come *on!*" Angus swung the wand around, haphazardly, totally out of control. "And Myriad, you didn't really answer Belle's question; where were you when we left Vixonight's house the other night? Were you really in William's pocket? His Mum washed those trousers, *y-o-u'd h-a-v-e b-e-e-n d-r-o-w-n-e-d….*" Angus was now completely out of his depth. The wand was far too powerful for him and as he swung it higher and higher, it seemed to get larger and larger and heavier and heavier. Angus's cheeks puffed out under the strain.

"Okay, if you *must* know, I was stealing *this!*" Myriad pulled a book from his back pocket and flicked it open. The book seemed to fall at any old page, and as the trembling elf repeated the golden words which flickered within, *"Vereculum Bonazetum Sponoferite!"* the wand forced Angus's tightly clenched fist to tap itself hard eight times on the floor. Angus flew violently about, his body thwacking against the hard floor at every move. He felt rather sick. Then, Myriad simply clenched his eyes shut tight. "You lot too, shut your eyes, and NO peeking!"

"Is that wand actually *yours?*" William shouted fretfully, his eyes pounding beneath their lids.

"Urr, no, not really..." Myriad shouted in reply as they all shot spiralling downwards, Angus's hair bolt upright "...but Priscilla made it look so frightfully easy."

"Who's Priscilla?" Alyssa cried out as they all fell, tumbling, into a dark crusty brown abyss. "Is she a magician? Is she a w-w-w-w-itch?"

"No, she's my Mother." Myriad thudded to the floor. "Ouch!" He rubbed his elbow. "Self-taught bewitched lady. Turned me into a stoat once, quite by accident, took more than an Anoukan week to get me back to being, well, me. Never had seven toes on each foot before that spell though. Never mind."

"Not filling me with any more confidence, Myriad!" William cried back. "Hope your magic's better than your Mother's?" William was still spinning through the air, and although Myriad had grounded, William just floated, unable to get down.

"That I can't tell, it's the first time I've tried!" Myriad sounded as horrified as everyone else, if not more. Then thud. They all found the floor. On top of Myriad. "Bbbbfbbbgbgbgbbbbg…"

"Where *are* we?" Angus choked as he inhaled the biggest cloud of dry old soil. "What on earth *is* this place?" He stood up.

"Relief!" Myriad could breathe, and his tiny nostrils let out an enormous wind far too loud for the elf to have made. "Oh, I thought I was going to die there for a second. Your fat behind over my mouth."

"It's beautiful." Alyssa looked mesmerised as she looked around.

"Angus's fat bottom cheeks, over my face? I think you'll find that's *not* beautiful." Myriad's body shook at the thought.

"What took you?" Belle suddenly appeared from nowhere. She drank purple berry juice from a crystal goblet and the most serene silver lake glistened behind her.

"Belle, how *dare* you run off like that! Don't you realise we should always act with caution? Especially now. Idiot." William shouted at his sister in a harsh whisper.

"Errr, remember your words?" Angus tried to remind William of before.

"Get lost…"

"Lizards never change their spots…" Angus turned to Belle.

"Leopards," Belle shook her head.

"Monkeys to you too." Angus replied.

"You're such a fool."

"Whatever. He loves you really. He cried at school, you know..."

"I said GET LOST!" William glared at Angus.

"He did, he cried you know, said he didn't care about you sticking out your tongue, and you could snub your nose at him any time AND he'd share his…" Angus leant in "…..share his chocolate."

"Now, I don't believe you at all, Angus!" Belle just chortled. "Not at all."

"Myriad, where *are* we?" William span around just as he saw the long winkle-pickered shoes of the elf disappear into the calm waters.

"Hello, hello, who have we here then?" A crimson ruffled dress hastened towards William, but he could not see who on earth was making it walk and talk. Then, a mass of orange matted hair appeared, and little chubby hands at the end of plump arms brushed the thick hair apart revealing a freckled pale face. "Who have we got here? What delightful friends has my son brought home for tea now? Belle and I have already met, and I knew we were expecting more as my kitchen string of lights flashed up all sorts of colours." The lady leant in. Her eyes peeled. "Quindig fixed them up, they don't generally work." Priscilla whispered the last part with an enticing chuckle, then clicked her fingers and stared at the crowd in front of her.

"Hello," William replied, politely, to the tiny rotund lady newly in their presence. "Phew, so you've found my sister. Thanks." The appreciative boy ruffled Belle's hair, still shaking his head in disbelief at her disobedience.

"Cretin," Belle scowled.

"*Quindiiiiiiiiiiig, Quin*dig, set more silver for teatime, please, and where *is* that Myriad now? He's always just disappearing off at mealtimes. Quindig, go find your son, dear. Quindig, are you listening?"

"Yes, dear," a supposed Quindig replied from somewhere nearby.

The chubby lady, who William presumed must be Priscilla, called out as a wild-haired scraggy looking tall man poked his pointy chin, followed by a triangular shaped nose and huge emerald eyes, out from an oval door carved into a moss covered hill (that turned out to be a tree house) across the shimmering lake waters, and the most whitest of white sailboats floated silently towards the children.

"Hop on then now," Priscilla ushered, herding first William, pulling Belle tightly by his side, and then Angus and lastly Alyssa at the rear. The shore on which they had all once stood turned into a distant sand bank, and Myriad leapt out the lake on board.

"That was refreshing! Hello Mamamamamama," Myriad grinned, and dripped all over the boat's floor.

"Oh for the love of all the earth, get dry before you get out of the water," Priscilla muttered to her son, which made no sense at all to those already on board.

"That's impossible," William looked dumbfounded.

"My type of woman, I like it," Angus flirted.

"Oh, not again," Belle just tossed her hair.

Myriad lay down on deck. Then, he dried between each of his thin, overly-long toes which did not match his tiny legs at all. He dripped his wet hair on his Mother's skirts and then threw his towel overboard. Quite ridiculous. He skidded up to the boat's helm. Myriad wasn't a timid little elfin creature at all. "Come on, let's go faster! What's the hold up?" and the seemingly shy little elf now tossed his meekness behind, grabbed the weirdest wheel William had ever seen, and heralded the boat towards the grassy meadow shores. "Home!" He crashed. Quindig fell overboard and Priscilla, well, she was just a mess. Covered in weed, her clothes became transparent. Myriad, he just nipped off the wooden raft before it even touched land. "Papapapapapapa!"

Quindig grinned. Wet.

"Hello Father!" Myriad climbed his Father's leg, grasping his greying beard and resisting, but losing, a familiar tickle. "Ah, Dad, leave it out!" but the struggle helped less and less.

"Myriad, Myriad how you've grown!" the oldish man chuckled.

"Yes dear, he runs off and simply shoots up in height and only seems to come home when he has a rumble in his tummy." Priscilla tried to sound cross.

"Why not? A rumble in my tummy is the best sound of nature." The elf rubbed his bare skin as if he hadn't eaten in days, and batted his eyelids at Priscilla. She fell for it, every time, but tried not to make it appear so.

"Myriad, my *dear*, where *have* you been and what *have* you been up to this time, and pray, *what* is that you are so awkwardly hiding behind your back?" Priscilla enquired with her brow increasingly wrinkled.

William got the impression that Myriad was a bit of a tearaway but simply terrible at covering his tracks. "Mrs, er Mrs..." William stumbled over how to address Myriad's Mother but her interruption ceased any further embarrassment.

"Please, dear, call me Priscilla, they all do," and at that, a collection of other elves, all dramatically resembling Myriad, poked varying pointy noses and long toes out from inside the tree house walls.

"Blimey, Myriad, are these all your brothers and sisters? What an enormous family!" William spoke out in disbelief.

"Yeah, yeah, that's them. Loadsa them. Loadsa them. *Everywhere*. So, how Priscilla even notices *I've* gone beats me," Myriad tut-tutted towards his Mother.

"I have my ways and means, you should know that by now," Priscilla retorted.

"He calls her Priscilla," Belle whispered to William. "He calls his own Mother *Priscilla*."

"Come in, come in, stop all of this nonsense. Really Priscilla, does it matter?" Quindig back-chatted his wife and William could tell that was probably a normal occurrence. He turned to his guests. "Priscilla, my dearest of wives, always makes enough food for the entire realm of Anouka, mind..." he cocked his head. "....most are in hiding these days." Quindig burst out into the randomest of characters. He held his head even lower. And blubbed until he was standing up to his knees in his own bubbling tears.

"Hiding from *who*?" Angus started to cry himself.

"Angus, you *know*..." Belle shot him an awkward glance. "Oh Quindig." Belle put her arm around the blubbering little man. "We know. You don't need to say. Myriad has explained. He's been with us, you see. Such a help. Such a gallant brave little elf. You should be proud." Belle praised Myriad so hard he did a little dance, and then stuck out his tongue at the third elf in line of too many to count. The third elf stuck out his tongue back. And the fourth, and then the fifth, it was like a show. And the tongues? They were silver and covered in spots. "Oh!" Belle tried not to look too shocked.

"See, Mamamama, Priscilla, I'm a *dream* of a son."

"Mmm, we'll see about that." Priscilla continued to try and see what her tearaway of a boy was still clutching behind his back.

"Oh, he's a *dream*, indeed. We *all* love Myriad," Belle continued. Fazed. Myriad just blushed in return.

"Phew, thanks Belle," Myriad chuckled, Belle could see he was waving the wand behind his back. It was letting off minute sparkles of scarlet dust; the trail delicately wafting up her nose.

"*Myriad!!!*" Belle whispered into the elf's ear. "Myriad, have you secretly saved yourself by sprinkling lie-enhancing dust up my nose?" But Myriad did not answer. He was just pleased he did not have to explain his obvious expedition this time. "*Tea-leaf!!!*"

"But the wand, it helped you out of *that* scrape, didn't it?" the elf pointed his nose back in the direction of a deep whirling hole in the sky through which Belle realised they must have fallen. "You know, the trees, ummmmm, killing you all?"

"Guess so."

Priscilla just smiled. She knew her son too well. So, she chose to ignore him. "Dears, dears, Anouka has heard of you, William, and Rosabella here." Belle gagged at the sound of her name. Priscilla turned and smiled at her. Belle had already helped herself to a very large serving of blueberry loaf with an enormous spreading of creamy yellow butter on top.

"Mmm, divine," Belle nodded through her filled lips. Her eyes glazed over in food glee.

"Belle, don't be such a glutton..." William tried to stop his sister from being sick. "Sorry, Priscilla, my sister, she's such an embarrassment."

"Willlliammammaaaaaaa," Belle scoffed another enormous slice. William looked at her. He rolled his eyes.

"How can we help, really though? I understand *She* has an accomplice, a helper in disguise who's rampaging about our school. We need to find out who that is, and follow it. Perhaps that will lead us to *Her*, but...that's all we can offer." William tried to lean in to the table to block his sister's face. It was stuffed full. "Belle," he whispered at her. "Belle? You're going to be sick," he tried to speak with a smile on his face and make his words come out as nice as possible. "Really, sisters, eh? Who'd have them?" he tried to laugh alongside his embarrassment. Seven, or was it eight, other elfin sisters popped up at the sound of their names.

"Sisters?" the elfins rolled the words off their tongues.

"Oh God, you're so not going to be more sisters for me," William groaned. The elfin-sisters all batted their glittering eyelashes at this large new boy. He was quite weird, really. Small ears, short toes and only five on each foot they realised as they tried to find more inside his shoes.

Priscilla listened. She had not even noticed Belle's gluttonous table manners. She was far too used to it herself. Her tribe of children sat on beanbags around the table. Purple jellies and black ice creams and weird stodge which resembled stinking mud fell everywhere. Priscilla sliced an apricot sponge, with minute precision in stark comparison to her offspring, by the mere flick of her emerald wand. Myriad looked in his hands. He no longer had the wand. His Mother just waggled her stubby little finger his way. She sighed. "There *is* another way, but it's just a myth."

"Anything will do. Let's try anything, well?" Angus piped up with a longing desire in his tone to just get on with things. He sounded quite anxious indeed.

"Angus, we can't simply do *anything*. Listen to Priscilla. Don't be so impatient." Belle frowned. She set Angus straight. He was not really amused.

"So-r-r-y," Angus scowled.

"The myth, it tells of a young boy born into Anouka many years ago," Priscilla cleared her throat. "Well before my time." All the faces gathered around.

"Ooooh, a story, Priscilla," the tiniest of the tiny elfins popped up.

"Yes, darling," Priscilla smiled and covered the ears of her baby elfin. "He was savoury and kind and so well liked by everyone, this boy. His sister? She was not. She was born with an evil streak, an evil streak just like at the very beginnings of Anouka when one young boy nearly turned against himself in a weird experiment gone wrong. She was upsetting all who crossed her. Some say she was just jealous of her elder twin, his likeability and his aptitude, but she did nothing about it, never even tried to mend her ways, never at all. She fell into a deepening gaping black hole one day and, she never returned. Inside the hole she came upon a book, a leather bound spell book, and as her brother attempted to save her she cast a spell upon him so severely from that book turning both herself into the Black Witch and her wholesome brother into a werewolf. He never returned home, and the Black Witch created the dark side of Anouka. The boy? He was never found. And the black hole? It was sealed up for eternity." Priscilla shivered. "More sugared almonds?"

"Yes, please…" but William snatched away the bowl from his greedy sister before she was finally sick.

"Vixonight," Alyssa whispered. "It must be him." She looked at William who held her gaze.

"Vixonight?" William replied beneath his breath. He rolled his eyes and looked around. He was confused. He feared Vixonight. How could he not?

Priscilla started to jitter about on the spot. "*Afyniad?*" Priscilla looked sternly at one of the other little elfins who appeared to be secretly looking guilty. "Afyniad? What do you have to say for yourself?"

"Sorry, Mama. I *do* need the toilet, and I will stop hopping on one foot procrastinating next time."

"We've all heard that before," another little spritely, more gnome-looking, voice interrupted.

"*You* did it when *you* were little, and you still *are*. I'm taller than you." Afyniad rattled back in defence.

"Priscilla?" William quietly asked. "Priscilla, do you believe this tale?"

Priscilla looked up from swishing her wand, rather ungallantly, around the table to try and make the used dirty crockery wash itself without such luck, and replied. "Yes, my dear, what did you say?"

"Do you believe the myth? The myth you just retold, do you believe it?"

"Me? Do I believe ancient tales? Well, I'm one to try anything once, and if that includes having faith in tales, well so be it, dear." Priscilla was quite something. "Oops, sorry Quindig, I shall have to perfect my wand swishing and swashing. I seem to somehow have turned your hair quite a nice shade of indigo. Rather suits you mind."

"Priscilla, really, don't get the boy's hopes up." Quindig joined the conversation, his hair changing from indigo to mauve then to a gross hue of pink. He stoked the silver crackling fire in the rounded corner of the room. Days were hot but nights were nippy. William looked at Priscilla to see her reaction. She ignored Quindig's lack of hope.

"Quindig, I could say the same to you. How can you deny what you cannot disprove?" Priscilla looked annoyed. William had provoked a debate.

"Oh dear, I'm not trying to cause trouble. I just need to know. We have to stop her, you know, the Black Witch, we must, really we must," and William realised perhaps he should know what to do. But he didn't. Anouka needed to be saved from being overturned into the ultimate dark side for eternity. He had absolutely no idea what to do. "Well?"

"Dear dear, let's sleep on it," and Priscilla seemed to glide across the uneven tiled corridor and pass through an enormous round hole, which just fitted her figure, to press new blankets onto an array of beds which plainly appeared in mid-air. "There, rest for the night and we'll talk come morning."

"And we've got time for that? To sleep?" but the large lady ignored William, and tapped each bed in turn. A sack of potatoes, seven ostriches and a pail of old washing up water collapsed from the ceiling.

"Oh…Mmmmmmm…Quin*diiiiiiig*? Come sort this mess, please?" She turned to the wand. "And I'll be having words with you later." Morning could not come quick enough for William.

The Water's Edge

"Belle, Belle wake up." William shook his sister's shoulders. Belle did not stir. "Belle!" He shouted this time. "It's snowing! Wake up." This time Belle did wake up, but she just rubbed her eyes and slowly pushed back the heavy feather filled bedclothes. She yawned, and then rolled over back into her land of nod. "*BELLE?*" The bed covers, they had not been like that last night, just thin little potato sacks. Quindig had not managed to reverse the spell. He just removed the potatoes, filled the sacks with the ostrich feathers, the ostriches still attached but he prayed for them not to move, and hoped that his wife did not notice.

Finally Belle came around. "William, where *are* we?" Overnight, the moss-cocooned tree house had floated miles downstream, and through the thin glass paned window just white skies and silver waters remained.

"Not sure, but get up. Angus and Alyssa aren't in their beds." William quivered in the cold. The top window in the bedroom was open ajar, just enough to let in huge flurries of crystal-shaped snow. The air was silent, eerily silent, and the siblings just stared out into the ebb of wintriness.

Belle pushed one long slender leg out from beneath her covers and immediately retracted it back inside. "What is *that?*" Her bed covers were moving. She had disturbed an ostrich who did not seem happy to have been woken up so abruptly. She shivered. "William, it's freezing. What on earth has happened? What happened to the soaring heat? It was more than enough to prevent myself collapsing into the waters in Myriad's steps yesterday but now, look, my lips are blue. Are they blue? They feel it." Belle looked into the octagon-shaped mirror. "And I can see icicles hanging from the mirror frame." She peered closer. Sure enough, the large glassed mirror hanging above the fireplace was dripping with sharp pointy ice, and the grate beneath simply black with dry crumbly charcoal seemingly not stoked for a while.

"Quindig, Quindig dear? Gracious, you are becoming more and more like Myriad every day. Where are you now? Quin*diiiiiiiiig?*" Priscilla shouted louder. "QUINDIG!"

"Cor, she's feisty this morning," and Angus hopped in through the space at the top of the open window, letting in an enormous trail of hail as he squeezed through the gap. "Brr, freezing out there!" and he flung a thick fur coat across the room to land with a hefty thud on his well slept in ruffled bed, that still just hovered above the gravelly grey floor. An ostrich poked out its head, disturbed by the coat landing right on its webbed feet. "What is *that* thing?"

"Oh, just an ostrich," Belle threw away his obviously banal comment. "Angus, where have you been? And why are you coming in through the window? Are you mad?" Belle looked at the weather. "Where's Alyssa, and where did you find *that* old thing?" She gestured to the brown matted pile of fur which Angus had thrown across the room causing Belle to duck.

"Hold your hoooooooooorses!" Angus collapsed onto Belle's bed next to her as he jumped in; a bit too cosy for William's liking. He looked rather too familiar in his surroundings. "*That* coat? Priscilla gave it to me. Alyssa has one too, but she's still too busy outside. Engrossed in Myriad's stolen spell book for hours, she's been."

"What do you mean, for *hours?*" William stepped forward.

Angus lay down. "You've been sleepy heads, it's past midday, you know." Angus nudged Belle quite deliberately hard on the shoulder and she tipped over backwards into her bedclothes. "I woke early, couldn't believe that winter was out there. Thought I was dreaming I was back in Arbrooth, I did." Angus held out his hand and pulled Belle back upright. "There, sorry lass." He smiled in jest.

Priscilla glided past the opening to the room, then teetered back and peeped inside. "You're awake, sleep is what you needed, can't have you investigating myths in a tired stupor, can we now? My 'Sleep State Spell' worked this time around, that's a blessing, must be getting so much more proficient in my old age." Priscilla glided in beside William. She did look much older, blimey, and so did Myriad.

"A spell? You cast a 'Stay Asleep Spell' on Belle and I?" William looked stunned. "You can't just do that!"

"That I did. Worked wonders, you do both look refreshed that's for sure." Priscilla clenched her emerald wand, giving it a warming kiss before moving aside to let Myriad come past.

"Myriad, what *has* happened? You're, well, so grown up? How long have we been asleep, Priscilla?

Myriad looks like, well, a teenager, an adult even, well, a small, elfin adult if that's possible?" William looked concerned, and he turned to Priscilla. "Well?"

"Don't worry, don't worry, see for yourselves, look in the mirror. You humans, *you* shan't age here in Anouka. We just sometimes do overnight, no rhyme nor reason, just wake up a little older, occasionally even younger, some mornings. I like those mornings." Priscilla smiled at Quindig who walked past the oval-shaped window outside. "*There* you are, *far* too elusive these days, and aloof by and by."

"Blimey riley, he's ginger! Quindig, he's got youthful ginger hair," Belle cried out in astonishment. "Not a grey strand to be seen. And no beard at all, and his skin..."

"*Strawberry blond*, I *do* much prefer strawberry blond, not ginger, dear," Quindig's youthful, deep, far from old and gravelly, voice replied.

"YES! I've found it!" Alyssa appeared beside Quindig. "I *knew* it, I just *knew* it. There was something that mystified me after I fell into the Black Witch's lair last summer. I didn't think about it at the time, just wanted to escape, but when I got home all I could think about was her flinching. Her eyes always seemed to divert away from any light. The tiniest chink of daylight and the Black Witch, she cowered into the corner. See, here, Vixonight's book, page 933 suggests that: *"Any such light, any representation of happiness and the eternal bright light of day, will cause evil creations to simply burn up in their own demise. Sunlight especially, and the heat that it brings, it will dramatically reduce any sordid witchery to utter shreds..."* Alyssa read from the spell book. "So, perhaps the intense autumn this year has been brought on by Vixonight trying to outwit his twin?" Alyssa looked around at the unsavoury freezing conditions. "His power isn't lasting, is it? We must go, we must start to help." She looked at Angus's relaxed composure. *"Well?"*

"Woah, where are we off to now? You mean *now?* We have to go right now, as in immediately? I was just getting used to this all you can eat buffet selection in the kitchen, see for yourselves. Come on, get a life. I've never seen such a spread." Angus's eyes lit up with greed, and he pointed into the kitchen which had turned into a vast canteen hosting everything. Drinks were every colour of the rainbow, and the food just indescribable. Fancies of cream delight, jelly shapes galore, and the most immense tower of exotic fruit imaginable, and that was just on the first table. "Can't we just stay for a little longer, *pleeeeeeease?*" questioned Angus. "No rush, is there?"

"No rush?" Alyssa cast a look of horror in Angus's direction. "Our home is about to be shot to the ground by the evils of a Black Sorceress, and all you can think of is the pit of your stomach? Angus Moon, you should be ashamed of yourself, really you should!" Alyssa looked completely horrified.

"Sorry." Angus blushed. He had been doing a lot of that lately. His head drooped. Not entirely innocently, but no one said a word. Then Angus gulped. "What the..." The tree house came to an almighty abrupt stop having started to whoosh off down a river at an almighty speed. It tipped up as far on its side as it could. William managed to lean out and grasp his sister's hand as she slid all the way from the upturned bed on which she sat towards the window Angus had left wide open. "William, Angus, help me?" Belle screamed and her voice warbled in terror as she neared the open window, her toes freezing as the waters came closer.

"*Grrrrr!*" a loud rumble emerged from the depths of the now deep silver oceanic waves and the largest shadow loomed from its depths. "*Grrrrr*! Belle, grab my coat, grasp my bristles and clench tight, now Belle? *Do* it, I can't hold onto you for much longer!" The awe struck child-like female obeyed the order from beneath the waters as her body started to sink. She shut her eyes until they were tightly closed. Silence. Belle no longer screamed. But instead, the deafening sound of the most gargantuan wave forced its terrifying weight over the top of the tree house crashing down and filling the bedroom with an icy cold torrent. Then silence. Placidity oozed. Calmness loomed everywhere. A strange unreal sense of serenity filled the immense gaping abyss where screams had once been. The waves ceased and the lake returned to a peaceful, yet dark, sheet of still water. It was too nonsensical to believe.

"Belle? *Belle?* Where *is* she? Who has *taken* her?" Angus panicked and ripped the crimson drenched curtains from their rail as he forced himself through the smashed jagged window pane. *"B-e-l-l-e?"* Angus's voice echoed through the purple mountain haze which approached, slowly, as if nothing had even occurred. "B-e-e-e-e-e-l-l-e?"

William felt sick. He rushed to the window and punched the glass with his clenched fist. The force of the impact struck out making his fingers bleed, but it worked and he made it out onto the mud stricken lawn. "Belle, where *are* you?" he cried in fear.

"Crivens indeed!" Angus leapt back. As William and Angus tipped their heads into the paradise haven silver lake, their own image in reflection did not stare back, but one of unequal measure.

"Heaven's above, the werewolf!" and William pulled Angus from the water's edge, both tumbling into the marshy crud beneath their feet.

"Grrrrr, boys, boys, boyyyyys." the brown hairy figure replied in a deep but calm safe sounding tone. "Do not fear me." The werewolf sounded tired.

"That myth. Heaven's above, only Priscilla," William heard Quindig mutter in a considerate chuckle behind him. "Oh Priscilla."

"You indeed are my saviour," Belle snivelled.

William had to rub his eyes free of ocean grit and disbelief as he viewed Belle kneeling down before a very ugly becoming werewolf. Belle patted the beast's shoulders and he actually purred in reply.

"William, did you hear that in fact? The werewolf purred at your sister. Go on, you next!" Angus gestured to William to touch the tame beast.

"After you, please. Be my guest?" William replied quite pale. He pinched his thigh to confirm it was actually real. "Seriously Angus, you introduce yourself first, my pleasure." William smiled to reassure his Scottish friend.

"Aye, ta," was all Angus could deem himself to say. "Ta, William."

"Pleasure," William replied. "Pleasure's all mine. As always."

Angus stepped forward. He cleared his throat. "Aye, Beast." He struggled for words, which was unlike him. "Aye, thanks for saving Belle," the Scottish boy spoke with disturbance in his voice. He did not like being, not nervous, but not in control of his surroundings. Talking to a werewolf seemed a little weird.

"Are you scared?" Belle whispered into Angus's ear. He could tell she was laughing.

"Na," Angus replied flippantly, not looking at Belle. But, despite his chiselled-faced exterior, Angus looked meek in the werewolf's presence, but the beast just nodded his thin gaunt coarse hairy head. Angus squinted, peering into the werewolf's eyes deeply." Are you okay?"

William listened, shocked at Angus's enquiry. He stepped in between Angus and his sister, but he just listened.

"I'm not too bad, considering," the beast replied.

"Considering what?" Angus stepped closer still, so close that he could feel the beast's hot breath on his cheek.

Belle stroked the beast's wet ebony nose.

"Beast, just get in here, come, for Heaven's sake, into the parlour here. Let's bandage that paw." Priscilla bustled through to intervene.

"It *is* you," Alyssa gasped. "It really *is* you. Vixonight?"

The beast roared, shaking the whole parlour. Ancient portraits of the elves' heritage fell from the crumbling walls, their images leaping from their frames. The beast's eyes rolled in their sockets as he stood still. The room continued to rumble, shudder and start to decompose around them.

"Vixonight, what's happening?" Alyssa cried out as painting after painting tipped from its nail and crashed to the floor, leaving only chippings of dust as evidence of their once existence. "Is this an earthquake?"

"I knew this day would come," Priscilla whispered in the lowest calmest tone the children had ever heard pass from her lips as they all watched hundreds of ancestors, once still life on portrait walls, flee to escape the calamity.

"Grandma, Great Uncle Todd, Miss Marshy! Come back!" Myriad called after his family who simply leapt from the shattered easels on the floor and dived out through the cracked windows into the mountain range beyond. "Aunt Ariella, Cousin Warbuckle?" But the translucent figures did not turn back.

"Priscilla, dear, I was unsure all these years whether to believe your tales or not." Quindig just shook his head. His wife looked quite calm considering her home was in utter chaos. The tree house had no roof, clean swept off in the storm, the window panes were blown right in and the family silver strewn every which way. The only article to remain intact was the spell book, still held tightly in Alyssa's firm grasp.

"Men, can't change their minds once they are destined to believe something quite the opposite. Dear Quindig, you disbelieved all that was headed our way through fear of its consequences. My dreams and belief in tall tales led me not to fear but to expect this day.

Come on, I'm prepared as always." Priscilla walked outside and, quite accustomed to her preparation, the most dramatic spell Myriad had ever seen his Mother cast happened before his eyes.

"I've been practicing this for *years!*" Priscilla cried. "Just never for *real!*" and the bumbling rotund lady created the most almighty splendiferous purple haze as far as the eye could see. "It's working! It's actually working!"

"Well I never." Quindig shook his head again. "Never should have doubted the old lady."

Enhancing the already mauve coloured sky Priscilla held her emerald wand high up to the Heavens and cracked the air magnificently three times shouting "*Nyzamtium, Plyborium, Jazelf!*" An enormous wave rose taller and taller from the ocean. Just as it surely could not possibly have risen much higher, the crest of the wave parted down the middle creating a huge crevice into which Priscilla dragged the beast. The others followed in silence; dragged in by an invisible vacuum.

"It worked! My spell to escape the Black Witch's winter actually worked!" Priscilla cried with glee. "Quindig, you believe me now? The tales I've been harping on about, the tales I've been waiting to occur, the old fashioned myths you were never to believe. They've happened. Good job we kept your Mother's dusty old wand." Priscilla smiled, whispering the last bit. "*Hold t-i-g-h-t!*" Priscilla shouted as the ocean walls grew taller still, and thinner until surely they were to disappear altogether, causing the tiniest line of people drowned in its shadow to walk single file; the water lashing at their puny shoulders.

"Oh my goodness, Priscilla, we're back *here!*" William cried, shocked.

"Where's here?" Belle cried in return.

"Back at the top of the old oak tree, the day I fell," William muttered under his breath. "Look, there's our cottage, the wisps of smoke as always masking the sky above the chimney. It's pretty damn dark now."

"Arbrooth just seems quite absolutely normal these days." Angus Moon shook his head. It was spinning. "Oh Arbrooth."

The old oak tree shook. Its roots pulled up mounds of cracked dry soil beneath. "We're going to fall. Grab a branch!" William screamed.

"Not this time." Vixonight gnarled. "I shan't let us fall this time."

"But you weren't with me the last time, none of you were." William frowned.

"You tumbled, blacked out, banged your head," Priscilla replied. "You didn't know anything. Naribu spoke with you as you fell. He explained the Black Witch's plight, but you saw nothing. Now, we can really begin!" Priscilla looked plum in the face with excitement.

"What are you talking about? Really, none of you were even up the tree with me. Yesterday, I really honestly was alone. Not even Belle was here, were you?" William looked at his sister for an explanation. She just shrugged.

"I don't know anything anymore," Belle whispered. "But I do know that we can now confront the Black Witch. Look at our numbers, our powers."

"England, it's just weird," Angus stood on the wobbliest branch of the lot.

"Dear William, Naribu blotted your mind of anyone else in your presence when you fell. If you had been privy to all of us, then you would not have tried to help, you may have even fled from this beast here." Priscilla pointed to Vixonight. "We do not know how you would have reacted sat up here on a branch with a blood

135

fanged werewolf, a terribly large elf and her family, and various pupils. If you had fought us, we would not be here now, escaped from Anouka to face the Black Witch when she calls for winter sports day right down there." Priscilla pointed awry, spiralling her wand to the ground far below.

"Whatever," Angus groaned. He was tired of trying to make out what on earth hold Anouka had on them. "When's tea?"

"William Joy, come down this instant before you fall!"

"Mrs Lovett!" William looked down.

Mrs Lovett shouted her demands across the school playground. "And I mean *this instant*. What are you looking at up there?"

Naribu flew past. He winked. The snowy white owl drifted plainly into view, mesmerising William and guiding him down to the ground swiftly in his arms. William landed softly. Mrs Lovett ran up.

"William? Nod if you can hear me? Squeeze my hand." Mrs Lovett peered into the boy's eyes and he sat up. Vixonight scarpered inside the school's dark dining room. Myriad, followed by his parents, cowered behind the old oak tree, and Belle closely guided by Alyssa and Angus, still moaning, towered over William.

"Anyone got any chocolate? I'm starving." William's tummy rumbled. He licked his lips.

"My sentiments exactly. Stand back. I'll help him up, Miss," Angus offered.

"And who are *you?*" Mrs Lovett turned to face Angus in bewilderment.

"Angus Moon. I'm new." He chuckled at having outwitted the teacher. That was a notch for his headboard.

"Mr Vixonight. Mr Vixonight?" Mrs Lovett stretched her head tall to try and see over the sea of heads. "Mr Vixonight, the new boy has arrived, from Scotland, remember? Alyssa will show him around. Alyssa?" Mrs Lovett shouted over her shoulder. "Alyssa?"

"Yes, Miss. I know." Alyssa ran up, breathless. She grinned and introduced herself to the new boy. "Alyssa Fellstrop." She shook his hand. "Pleased to meet you."

"Angus Moon. And you're friendly," the broad new Scottish boy replied, and all the pupils, pushing forward trying to get a look in, cupped their hands over their mouths cracking up at the new boy's funny accent.

"Alyssa, really. You've gone scarlet." Mrs Lovett was not amused.

"Where's he from?" Isla whispered in Robyn's ear.

"Somewhere far from here," Robyn whispered in return. "That's for sure."

The Mirrored Wall

"This is surreal." Angus encouraged everyone to walk faster. "Do you think we'll see ourselves by the pond, where we were before, you know, when that goblin surfaced?" Angus sounded cocky and far too confident for Belle's liking.

"Angus, we get it, we really do. I know we're reliving yesterday and our trip home from school, but the advantage of hindsight is not to take advantage. Do YOU get it?" Belle could not help put Angus in his place.

"What's got into you, Belle?" Angus spun around from well ahead of her. "Why are you so cautious? We know Vixonight is on our side, we know that for sure, so let's have some fun. That goblin can just go to hell for all we should care."

"Angus! If you don't stop, I swear..." Belle raged. "If this is how you acted back in Arbrooth then, well, I'm not sure I like you. Just go back. You keep talking about it. What if we run into our other selves from yesterday? I have no idea what a parallel universe would do, so let's not go looking for trouble." Belle shook her head

139

once more. "Although I know that's what you do. You're sounding more like that elf every hour."

"But it's fun!" Angus mooched.

Belle's distance from Angus was enough to curb his bravado and he slunk back further, but only a little. The sun set low, and the village meadow pond loomed. A door out of the corner of Belle's eye crept open and Miss Terrine came out of her flint-stacked cottage. Her garden was wild, quite messy and wrought with climbing ivy, and her windows just filthy, thick with grime and fresh brown gloopy mud.

"I didn't know Miss Terrine lived there?" Belle spoke under her breath. "In fact, I've never seen that ramshackle old cottage before. I guess I'm too consumed sometimes to even notice my own surroundings." Belle had perked up.

Angus moved a little closer. Belle twisted her shoulder high so as to block his face. "What's up?" But Belle pretended not to hear.

"I didn't know where she lived to tell you the truth. Just that she survives only for painting and water colours, not to mention her wild antisocial gardening crafts. It's a right mess. Look at the stench on her front lawn. Disgusting." But before William could finish his sentence a dark shadow loomed above and a straggly murky covered figure passed close over-head turning the succulent green grass to thin dry brown sticks. Then, it disappeared into the damp crevice within the old oak tree.

"That was the goblin. The Black Witch's accomplice just fled past us. Just like yesterday. It didn't try and get us, I wonder why not?" Angus asked out loud.

"The Black Witch needs us alive," Alyssa replied in a loud shaky whisper. "And look, *he's* here, look." Alyssa pointed into the pond's thick reeds, and they shook as Vixonight crept about and slunk low. "I guess you didn't see him the last time?"

"No. That's why the goblin fled, eh? It clocked Vixonight. I just flew into the air from fear. I shan't forget that." Angus trembled at the thought.

"Where's Miss Terrine?" Belle peered across the road to where their formidable thin-lipped, quite banal looking in appearance, teacher once stood. Her overgrown garden weeds swayed violently in the wind and, despite the soaring heat, droplets of ice had begun to form on the window panes and paint peeled from the front door. "She's disappeared. How odd. There's no way she could have passed us without us noticing."

"Yep, she's pretty noticeable, no quibbling there," Angus muttered as he pictured the less than attractive lady. He mooched along the road. "Don't think I've ever seen anyone so ugly."

"Perhaps she went back indoors, when we weren't looking? When we were shocked by that goblin?" William looked about.

The children stood there. They all thought the same. Their eyes widened, and they froze to the spot. Angus was the first to open his mouth.

"Her? Miss Terrine. The goblin? But she's far too tall and she's been at your school forever. And anyway, she was over there." Angus pointed to Miss Terrine's tumbledown cottage and murky wet garden strewn with pond life and algae. "When the goblin passed over our heads, Miss Terrine was plainly right over there." Angus waved his arms into the air all around. "She can't be in two places at once. I can't begin to get my head around this."

"You can flirt, no problems there," Belle sniped at Angus.

"Aye, aye, got it now. That's why you're so uptight. Jealous," Angus chuckled.

"Am not, you take that back. You're too full of yourself, you are." Belle marched off. "As if I'd be interested in you? You're stupid. We've just been talking with elves, seen atrocious spells cast, and liaised with a talking werewolf. So why does Miss Terrine's inability to be in two places at the same time shock you? You *are* stupid. I'm going to look inside her house." Belle was practically across the road when, quite abruptly, for no reason at all, she fell to the floor. "Ouch!" Belle was flat on her face. She felt in front of her. Instead of just the air around her there appeared a hard translucent wall. A see through barrier which prevented her from going any further just fixed itself into the road. "Guys, there's a wall here, built right here. I can't get to Miss Terrine's cottage." Belle squinted behind to the pond and its murky waters, then back to the marshland of their art teacher's garden. "Oh my goodness, it's a mirror! Miss Terrine's house and garden are just a reflection from the pond. Not a precise reflection, but what we are made to see. Miss Terrine, *she must* be the goblin! We see her in disguise, what this wall shows us, but the pond, and the goblin rising from it, tells the truth. Miss Terrine came out of her house just as the goblin escaped over us. This wall is a mirror.

Cunning. Clever. Reflections reflected as they wish to appear."

"Where's her cottage then? It's not by the pond. There's no cottage there." Angus tried to outwit Belle. He did not like being in the dark, not understanding.

"Don't you see, *Angus*?" Belle snubbed him. "The mirrored wall shows us what it wants us to see. The Black Witch needs us to see Miss Terrine, her home, her garden. It has to reflect normality, not arouse suspicion, but in reality, who really passed us by was the goblin, living in those waters. It rose from the reeds just as Miss Terrine opened her front door." Belle spoke as she began to piece together what she saw. "Those reeds in reflection were her cottage."

"You're sounding as mad as Priscilla," Angus quibbled back.

"But she was absolutely right! Crackers or not, Priscilla was absolutely right when it came to old myths. Why can't *you* believe *me*? You're sounding like that Quindig. So sceptical." Belle retorted. "I'm right too, Angus Moon, you'll see." Belle stormed off towards home. "*Hopeless idiot*," she called back.

"She's proper angry with you, Angus!" Alyssa laughed.

"She's probably right. You know, Belle," William nodded at Angus. "She always is. But how we prove it and act normal around Miss Terrine at school? It beats me."

"Use this!"

Popping up suddenly from a hiding place amongst the dry cracked bottle-green reeds waving Priscilla's wand was Myriad. "She doesn't actually know I've got it, snuck it out her skirts as we tumbled down the old oak tree. Mind, she'll certainly know soon. She's forever practicing new spells, so we need to act quick."

"Oh Myriad! Someone normal and sane at last! This lot are driving me up the wall!" Alyssa hugged the elf, who blushed, and pointed up the hill towards Belle in the distance. She rolled her eyes at the boys. Then let go of Myriad. He fell to the floor and drew breath.

"I'm dying," Myriad muttered. "I'm crushed."

"Normal and sane?" Angus retorted. "That's a bit scary, Alyssa. If Myriad's normal we must be positively..."

"...Annoying, annoying and less than intelligent!" Alyssa finished moody Angus's sentence. "Can't you see? We need to act, think, be Anoukans now, abide by

145

its magic and just take whatever it throws at us. We can't dismiss the sorcery we need to outwit."

"Weirdo, aye. We're all doomed." Angus frowned, but despite his complete loss of words, inside he agreed. He certainly did not fancy living in winter all year. Arbrooth was testament to that.

"Okay. I give in, Myriad. Cast your spell. I suppose it's better than school anyway. Did you see that maths equation on the board? Like another language it was." Angus rubbed his stomach again. "And I'm still hungry. Perhaps we need to petrify Miss Terrine?" Angus sounded suddenly alert. "We better use this!" And the cunning Scottish boy pulled Vixonight's magic spell book from his threadbare school shorts. "See, not so stupid and bumbling after all, Alyssa." Angus smirked.

"Angus, where did you get that? It fell right out my pocket as we tumbled from the old oak tree. I've been meaning to own up, honestly." Alyssa looked embarrassed.

"Come on, no time for banter." Angus smirked further and he ignored Alyssa's question. Ice was starting to encrust further over the duck pond, and the mirrored wall was depicting a hard frosty covering on Miss Terrine's cottage in reflection. "That goblin must be with the Black Witch by now, telling her everything. She will know where we are."

"We can't stay together." William looked about. "The Black Witch's spell needs all four of us to succeed." He quivered at the thought. "Find a spell, quick." William spoke as a deep greying cloud loomed above the village and a horrendous storm seemed to whip up. In the distance, Belle screamed as Myriad smacked Priscilla's emerald wand on the hardened mud by his feet and Angus shouted out a formidable riddle that caused the ground to tremble.

"What are you casting?" Alyssa shouted above the cracks of thunder.

"Page 226, *'Turning the Black Sorceress to Stone.'* It seemed the best choice really." Angus shouted back.

"You've got the wrong page!" Alyssa grabbed the magic book whose pages flapped violently in the wind. "You're reading *'Create a Tornado Persay.'* Angus, we need to hold hands or we'll all be sucked into its epicentre. Angus! Hold my hand..." but as Alyssa cried out her words were lost to a tempest, and the children started to be forced into the eye of the storm.

"Verlicerous, Persinfergrate!" William cried back in complete shock.

"William, where did you learn that?" Alyssa caught his hand tight.

"No idea! It just came to me, just like that." William went pale with caution, but before he could begin to think what next to shout, thud, he landed inside the walls of a colourful garden, perfumed with scent and blooming with splendour. Alyssa and Angus thudded by his side.

"What on earth happened? Where are we?" Myriad thudded down in the luscious grass beside them. His wand bounced into the fir trees, and the magic spell book floated down into the centre of the foursome, all aghast with no knowledge of their whereabouts.

"Where in Heaven's name is this place?" Alyssa enquired in a faint mutter.

"Never, ever take my wand again, Myriad." Priscilla's most angry tone rang out from a white washed painted shed. "Good job I had my homing device set, and the *'Stay Asleep Spell'* along with the extra special *'Magic for the Needy'* still inscribed in William's mind, unbeknown to William, thank you." She tapped William's frowning brow with her handkerchief.

"This, Myriad, is *my* wand. Wherever it goes, I ultimately go too...to retrieve. What are you thinking of stealing it again, from your own Mother; despite your Dad wanting me to make his hair actually strawberry in colour, indeed what is he thinking? I need this wand more than you and your haphazard sorcery, Myriad." Priscilla did sound cross.

Myriad hung his head. "Sorry, Mama." He tried to look doe-eyed. "I really am. Just thought what with Vixonight's spell book and your wand I could try and save Anouka. I just wanted you to be proud of me." Myriad dropped his head even further to look at the floor, but his one eye stealing a glance upwards terminated his chances of any sympathy.

"Myriad, you mynx! You really nearly had me there! If it wasn't for that roaming infectious left eye of yours, really, dear son." Priscilla grasped her wand tight and shook her head. "My children, from whom do they inherit such deceit? Such a good job I could intervene and collect you from the eye of that crazy torpedo you had created, Angus. Mmm, I did a nice job relocating us all here." Priscilla looked around with a stupendous smile drawn onto her face.

"It's a tornado, Mother. Not torpedo." Myriad tried not to laugh and get on the wrong side of Priscilla yet again.

"Where, gracious, *where* is there a tornado?" Priscilla ducked and rushed back inside her white-washed garden shed as if the pine planks from which it was built would protect her.

"You said torpedo," Myriad replied. "Never mind."

"A torpedo, even worse, take cover, all of you!" and Priscilla tried to usher the beaming children, who held their sides in hysterics, into the small wooden hut. They would not fit. She tried to shove them in; Angus being the most problematic.

"Priscilla, there's no tornado and there is certainly no torpedo, they're gone." It was the only way to get the flapping lady to listen Angus tried.

"Oh, thank goodness, can't be doing with telegraph poles." Priscilla wiped her perspiring brow. Brushing her, now bright yellow, locks from her face, Priscilla coughed aloud. "That's not part of my spell," and she coughed again. "Just building up," and she plucked the spell book from Angus's sweaty palms and cleared her throat, for the third time in succession. The spell book pages seemed to flick impressively over and over totally independently. Neither Priscilla nor Angus were even close to the book, but Priscilla just stared harder and harder as the crinkled loose leaf parchment fluttered and skipped backwards and forwards as if it was actually being fingered to find the right chapter.

Priscilla held her emerald green wand high above her head and whispered a strange cocktail of words, words meaning nothing to its listeners. "Crypt-synxh byceum hocus praz, roxyn bravo mocus traz!" Nothing. Priscilla huffed. "That was *it!* I have muttered this verse for years, leaving out the exemplary shoes for good measure and ample success, of course." Priscilla repeated the bizarre concoction, this time tapping together the heels and toes of her crystalite footwear. "Crypt-synxh byceum hocus praz, roxyn bravo mocus traz!" and Belle fell down next to them with an almighty thud. "Oh yes, I think the spell thought you were already in our presence, sorry about that, dear. Nice to see you again."

Belle forced a smile while rubbing her bruised posterior. "It's nothing." She cringed.

"So, we're all here?" Priscilla counted her onlookers. Vixonight hung back in the bushes. His eyes were yellowing.

"Perhaps he still doesn't trust us?" Angus whispered to Belle, but she didn't return a reply. "Are you still holding a grudge? Well?"

"No, and ssh. Can't you see the concentration on Priscilla's face?" Belle replied, and she stood up to move places.

"Sit down, dear, sit down!" Priscilla frantically waved her arms. "Oh my Lord, don't come between my wand and the mirrored wall, Belle!" But it was too late. Priscilla had already flicked her heels with the wand and a great spark shot through the air, and through Belle, and she was taken back out through the mirrored wall to its ghastly tornado struck side.

"Oh Crivens and Cruvens, what *have* we done?!" bumbled Priscilla sounding far too much like Myriad.

"We?" William butted in.

"Oh dear, that was a *'Deletion Spell'*, known through history and passed down through my ancestry for centuries, but well, we don't really count on people getting in its way." Priscilla flustered flicking through Vixonight's spell book. "I was hoping to delete forever that brutal tornado, the one that still seems to be the other side of this here shimmering wall. But Belle? She's there too."

"Are you looking for how to correct your spell, Priscilla?" William asked worriedly. "Are you? That's the third time Belle has been sucked away!"

"Urr, yes yes, but we'll get there, don't fret about your sister." Priscilla did not sound at all convincing.

"Where exactly has she disappeared to?" Alyssa squinted at the bumbling woman. "And what exactly *is* the *'Deletion Spell'*?"

"Exactly as Mother says," Myriad replied. "Belle has gone." Myriad hung his head.

"Myriad, don't be so dramatic!" Priscilla whacked her son around the head.

"Ouch!" Myriad slunk off muttering. "Her wand has deleted the mirrored wall alongside anything in its path."

"Myriad, please, don't scare the children. So..." Priscilla turned to William. "My spell null and voided the wall and all its foreboding atrocities. Look, see, your village? Your school? All now revived, free from that dreadful winter storm. Marvellous, eh?"

"And the downside?" Myriad answered back again.

"Don't get me wrong, the Black Witch will track us down once again, her powers are stronger than mine, but I have deleted the onset of her sudden winter. I just didn't particularly plan on deleting Belle at the same time." Priscilla tapped her wand on the gravel.

"It's all your fault, Angus. If you hadn't upset my sister, she'd still be here now." William threw a handful of stones at the Scot.

"Hush child. Many a true word spoken in jest, I know, I know, but that doesn't help Belle now, does it? My spells have been working through you." Priscilla flicked a switch on her wand and looked around. "Why don't we rest up here for a while," she whispered and tittered and jiggled her legs quite inanely before a perfectly crisp white tablecloth floated down from the climbing ivy tree surrounding the walled garden allowing the surprised onlookers to see it spread with a marvel of treats. Glacé topped iced tarts bobbed in a diamanté cut bowl of ice cubes to keep them cool, butterscotch and heatherberry pancakes hovered in mid-air, and strangely shaped sausages danced on their plates, and fizzed loudly when Angus was the first to try and catch one.

"Ouch! That sausage actually burnt me! It hopped straight into my fingers and physically stung me viciously like a wasp!" Angus's fingers steamed, letting off a burning smell into the air.

"Don't be greedy then, Angus!" Alyssa laughed and teased. "At least wait for the chairs to be placed around the table before scoffing the lot!" The children watched as the dazzling tablecloth formed itself into a hexagonal shape and tall dainty silver chairs sat themselves neatly around it.

"Now you can dine, Angus dear," Priscilla gestured towards the heavenly spread laid out.

"What a treat!" Angus's eyes nearly popped out.

"I can't possibly eat a thing until I know Belle is safe," William scorned, just standing on the spot whilst Angus, Alyssa and Myriad tucked in. "And I don't know how you can either, Angus Moody-Moon?"

Priscilla looked up at William's saddened forlorn eyes from over the rim of her turquoise star-shaped spectacles. "All in good time, William, all in good time," the sorcerous lady replied, flicking through the spell book with such speed and poise William could not actually distinguish any single page. "My spells aren't known to last, so the mirrored wall could appear right back as clear as it vanished. It is the doing of the Xavishum after all." Priscilla only whispered her name. "If we find my spell to work and I have truly obliterated what did lie between us and the vicious tornado, well, this here should help us through if we need it." Priscilla tapped the pointed end of her wand onto page 9917 entitled *'Regaining a Lost One'* and nodded, quite seemingly in control. She tapped her wand four times. "Oh, my shoe has completely disappeared! And now it's popped up again on the other foot!" Priscilla hopped about with two shoes on one foot and a bare one showing knobbly short toes. Her toe nails were painted purple, no yellow, no orange? William tried not to understand.

"Your spell, working?" Myriad threw back his head, dropping the stickiest ever toffee pear onto the tablecloth which then immediately began to scrub itself independently with a pink sponge, hands protruding from a terracotta pot. "Mother, really!" and Myriad, growing taller but sounding equally as childish as the hours passed, teased Priscilla and pointed down to his extra toes. "Your spells, eh?"

"I was a novice then, Myriad. Stop scaring William and eat your peas," and before Myriad could dare to mention that no ghastly peas were actually present, an enormous bowlful of the greenest roundest, softest peas the elf had ever had the misfortune of seeing, complete with their own large copper spoon, appeared on his mat.

"Come on, eat up." Priscilla raised her eyebrows. The spoon did the same and dolloped mushy blobs of sickeningly awful tasting vegetables into the mouths of anyone endangered enough to be sitting too close to Myriad.

"Yes Mother," Myriad replied. He hated peas. He thought he was about to vomit.

As Myriad spooned pea after pea into his wide open mouth, which he could not get to close any smaller as his lips tingled awfully if he even tried to purse them shut, a jingle ensued. Under the table beneath his feet a small hard round clear ball kept rolling into his toes through his tough rope like sandals. "Mother, as if getting me to eat bowlfuls of hateful peas, that never seem to diminish in number as I inhale each mouthful, rolling balls into my feet is just the limit. Please just stop. I am sorry, so sorry, I stole your wand. Never again. I promise this time," Myriad whined.

"Myriad, dear, you must be mistaken, or my spell has a glitch somehow. I am not rolling balls into your feet. I am not *that* childish," Priscilla replied in a tickly, itchy voice, and glanced under the table colliding heads with her son as she too peered wide-eyed at the gleaming translucent sphere rolling backwards and forwards between the elf's feet. Then, a little voice inside crept into the air, and at first glance there appeared to be a figure inside the chiselled sphere. The little figure wore tiny clothes the same shape and shade as Alyssa, but had a scowling face that only resembled Belle.

"Blimey, she's in that glass ball!" Angus choked and shot forward to take a better view. "Belle, how on earth did you get inside there?" He found it hard to focus on her as she kept rolling away from him, then hurtling back in his direction.

"Don't worry about that!" the angry tiny tone just about made itself clear. "Just get me out and full-sized again! And please stop me rolling about like this! I am feeling quite sick." Belle began to turn a pale hue of grey as she felt a breath on the back of her neck. Xavishum appeared close behind, her scathing lips and black rough hob-nailed boots booming and shaking the glass interior causing Belle to fall and tumble onto the floor.

"I'm quite liking a little Belle! Less to cope with. This is fun!" Angus tormented the ball, laughing into the air and tossing it from hand to hand not realising Belle's fate. She pummelled on the thick curved glass.

"Angus!" Belle cried, looking rather faint. "A-N-G-U-S!"

"Little Belle, who'd have thought it? Aye, who'd have thought it?" Angus was in his element.

"Angus, you fool!" Belle hammered so hard onto the inside of the ball her fists hurt and purple bruises appeared immediately.

It was then Angus noticed who was on her trail, and he had not the slightest idea what to do. It was William who snapped him out of his tormenting mode. Angus was dumbstruck. William grabbed the glass ball in the palms of his hands, wrenching it from the dancing Scot. Belle stared at Angus's enormous green eyes hiding behind William from her side of the clear-chinked glass ball window-panes. His pupils appeared huge to Belle's small stature. "Make me big!" she demanded from inside, and it was all Angus could do but grin and watch the ball being passed to Priscilla.

"She wants to be big again Ms Priscilla!" Angus chanted, trying to look stoic. It did not wash.

"Cretin!" Belle cried, muffled.

Angus was still grinning like a Cheshire cat who had just gotten the last of the cream. "But you're a coward, you are!" Belle cried louder. "Look at me! Do something! Wipe that stupid smile off your face!"

"Hiccus ponchus mikel gnaff, snarzel perifocas bookus graff!" Priscilla sounded like she was actually being tortured, but she was cut short as the glass sphere grew and grew and rolled, uncontrollably, down the unlevelled garden towards the ginger orange brick built wall. It grew and it grew as it rolled, and then crash! The enormous glass ball collided with the bricks; the noise of a ton of glass breaking filling the air, and the sphere shattered into a million pieces.

"Awesome!" Angus slapped his thigh.

Belle tumbled free and stood up, her hair ruffled more than ever before, and her eyes quite giddy.

"I must have cast a *'Get Tiny spell'* not a *'Deletion spell'* by mistake," Priscilla muttered. "But by all accounts that turned out for the best. Right, Belle? Staying with us this time?"

"Yeah right, it wasn't my fault. It wasn't my intention to disappear…again. But, thank you, Priscilla." And the right-sized girl promptly fell right back down. A crimson booted-foot joined to an ashen leg lay beneath the rocky fallen brick wall by Belle's side.

"Xavishum!" Priscilla panted. She had only read about Xavishum in mythical books. "For the love of all Anouka, she *is* real," Priscilla muttered. "It's Xavishum! Run, Myriad, run!" But the entire group were stuck fast. Petrified to move an inch.

The Coming of Xavishum

"Xavishum. That was Xavishum?" William trembled, grasping one of the fallen bricks in his hand. He had never dreamed of mentioning her name. The Black Witch sounded far less daunting.

"Xavishum. That *is* her." Priscilla pulled Vixonight's spell book from the fourth layer of her purple skirted frock and flicked haphazardly through the chapters searching. "Here! Xavishum!" she murmured. "Just a myth? I don't think so. I *knew* you were real. Your serpent slaves are by your side, eh." Priscilla tensed. She had waited for this day. "Don't catch their dark glare kids, for Heaven's sake! The snakes, keep your distance. Keep running and don't look back!" Priscilla was yet to realise they were all just running on the spot getting nowhere fast. She could hear the cracking of the bricks from the dishevelled wall move as Xavishum pieced herself together and emerged into the garden. Everyone else kept on running, on the spot. The garden seemed endless. It probably was as they were never to get anywhere. Xavishum's serpents slithered, jesting cruelties and cackling at the stupidity of the sight before them. Xavishum's body grew taller and paler with extreme determination.

"So, you think you can be wise and cast spells on me, *do* you?" Xavishum muttered, spitting glass everywhere. Splinters fell from her hair and cut razor sharp slices through her clothes. Her aura filled the sky, turning it another shade of blue, a blue which was dark and cumbersome. "I knew your Father and their Fathers, Priscilla. They kept me at bay, kept Xavishum from entering into the light side of Anouka for years, but Krook has now found a way in; thanks to Alyssa. Xavishum is now here, and so nearly *nearly* the Queen!" Xavishum boomed and spoke of herself in the third person, roaring her incarnation so loud the garden walls fell completely into disarray. Xavishum's serpents slithered into the ground.

Then, one by one, the serpent's bodies pushed up the soil as they indecently homed in on their prey. "Sss!" A tone rang out from beneath the earth as the serpent master of the pack slimed orders at its followers. To Belle, Angus and Alyssa the sound of the swarm of filthy reptile behaviour just filled them with unknown dread, but William's ears grew more and more accustomed to the conversations each scaly buried serpent passed between another. The boy listened intently and shuddered at the transcript he heard.

"Back then, Greer was just a young boy, heralded for his bravery and helpful demeanor at home. His bitter sister, we like bitter and revengeful, was the loner. Not a vein even deep within her soul proved to care for her brother. The parents loved their children equally, but Greer's sister could only ever envisage his demise." The master serpent continued his tale whilst his novice servants hissed and squirmed under the pitted soil. The conversation grew lurid and demonic but William still stuck to the spot sinking in the wet earth listening to the entire tale. *"Sss, Verona, Greer's sister, planned to impale Greer, but fell deep within Krook and never returned home. She heralded her transformation into Xavishum, the eternal Black Witch, and her ditched attempt to kill her well-liked brother led her to depict him as a werewolf for eternity. Krook had given her an all-powerful reign. He can maybe never become Greer again, never relive his youth long lost centuries past, and only now has Krook found an opening to this new world. The Black Witch will soon take all of Anouka, light and dark, my faithful serpents, and only upon Xavishum's bloodshed will Greer prosper and return*

home. But until then, or if Xavishum casts any more vindictive spells upon her werewolf brother soonest, we will all prosper!"

William stood open-mouthed. Something brushed his shoulder.

"Vixonight!" William grabbed his mane. "Come on."

Vixonight was feeling weak. His sister's presence so close forced the strength from his soul and his orange fiery eyes seemed less than even dim.

"What is it? Why so lank?" William stared, for the first time, into Professor Vixonight's weary eyes. He looked shaken, worn out.

"I can't fight her much longer. She is not my sister, Verona, anymore. She betrayed all my family for greed and power long ago. We share no love. I have no sympathy. Her closeness is affecting my strength. Look, even my legs are losing the fight." Vixonight sank to the floor.

"No, this is ridiculous! Get up!" William shook the beast but clumps of his wiry black hair just fell into his fingers. "Surely you want to bring her down, Professor Vixonight? You *are* strong! You *HAVE* to be strong for all our sakes. Please?!" William pulled the tired werewolf along, desperately heaving the beast from sinking further into the black mud that grew thicker making it increasingly difficult to walk. William felt his arms weaken as he gritted and clenched his teeth, tightening his grip around the beast's mane. "Come...*on!*" William perspired but knew he needed to get Vixonight free. The bubbling soil was beginning to feel hotter around his ankles, and he could feel his feet harden into the sinking mass. "Come...*on!* Help me, Vixonight!" William shrieked this time. The serpents beneath the earth drew closer. The soil in which they thrived bubbled high. A crack of thunder in the sky ensued. "There *WILL* be bloodshed!" William cried to the deep reddening sky. "I swear we will defeat *you*, Xavishum! There will be bloodshed soon. *YOUR* blood! I heard it all!"

Vixonight slouched. His whole body weary. Then, as if by some demonic magic, the beast hauled his weight from the sinking mud. His deep voice roared as his eyes fired bright orange again. Nosing William up onto his rough bare back, the beast ran into the forest once more. "There *WILL* be the slaying of my sister, Verona!" the beast cried back, his words echoing to the skies. "*Rrrrrrrr!*"

"This way," a voice whispered from nowhere. "Psst, in here! No, look down, down here. No, *right* down here, William." William only managed to identify from where the tone arose as he saw the tip of Priscilla's wand in a hollow at the foot of one of a zillion fir trees sprouting out of the ground as far as the eye could see.

"Priscilla, what are you doing right down in there? Can you fit? Are the others with you?" William leant as far down into the fir tree's hollow without having to dismount from his ride. He patted Professor Vixonight. "Shall I call you Professor Vixonight?" William asked.

"If you like." The werewolf stretched his neck as high towards the fast disappearing white stars as feasible. His nose sniffed the fir tree's scent. He had remarkable senses. "If you like, that's fine with me."

The stars faded, the moon retreated and a silvery sun started its day. As the beast inhaled the last scent of a nearby everglade his wiry hair frizzled and his face shrank from a pointy dark animal visage to the svelte gaunt face of a middle aged man; the headmaster. "Now you know," Professor Vixonight quivered.

"Or shall we call you *Greer*?" William whispered, looking about and hanging his head as if saying a rude word.

The Professor stared at William, open-mouthed. "I have not heard that name in *centuries*. Not since I was a young boy," the man replied in a low unhappy tone. "How do you come to know my name? My *real* name?"

"Yes, William?" Belle jumped down her brother's throat.

"Gotcha!!!! My bumblings *do* have their upsides! He's still infected with my magic, and for that, William dear was able to understand the serpents' conversations. I did not hear it all. What did they say?" Priscilla whispered her final question. "Tell, William," she hushed. "Tell us."

William glanced around. They seemed to be safe.

"They shan't follow us here," Professor Vixonight replied. "Neither the Black Witch nor her serpent servants will come near that wand." The headmaster pointed to the, now quite dull-looking, magic wand in Priscilla's grasp. "They know that wand. It belonged to ancestors past of which Krook was the arch enemy. If we stay near Priscilla, our fate is not sealed."

"Please, please let this be some dreadful nightmare from which I am about to wake up! For the life of Arbrooth! Take me back!" Angus threw up his arms. "Ouch!" His arms had caught a prickly branch.

"Quintessential rural England, Mother said as I packed the last of seventeen suitcases and we trudged nine hours down south. I must look up that word, *quintessential*, when I get home. I am almost certain its definition is not this!" Angus looked towards the murky terrain from which he had escaped and cast his mind back to Xavishum and the beast. "Not using that estate agent again, for sure."

Belle was certain Angus thought all this sorcery and Anouka was quite normal for England. "Angus, I really wouldn't go blaming the estate agent, not quite yet anyway." Belle taunted, but she could not decide if Angus was just being facetious. She had never encountered such a dry sense of humour in a boy.

"What did Xavishum's serpents say?" Priscilla whispered again.

William pondered how best to retell what he had overheard. "The serpents, of which one was the master, hissed that until Xavishum's blood was shed, the Professor would not return to his boyhood, namely Greer. Our werewolf is called Greer. Simply a boy. Anouka would soon be hers. Xavishum, your hateful sister Professor, will prosper. But we can stop her. We have Priscilla's wand which they fear, man do they fear that thing, and Xavishum knows nothing of the knowledge I overheard. Don't you see? I'm privy to how Xavishum can be slain." William slunk down inside the hollow tree. Professor Vixonight followed.

"I see. We have inside knowledge," Priscilla chuckled in quite a deep voice. "Formidable, dear." Priscilla had a very clever underlying tone which William found incredibly easy to pick up.

"Priscilla? You sound like you have your own agenda?" William whispered solely into Priscilla's round ruby ear as close to her skin as possible. Priscilla could feel the boy's warm breath on her neck. "You're not here just to save Anouka, are you? Have you a personal vendetta? Have you?" William squinted deep into Priscilla's eyes. There were plenty of thoughts in her head, he knew.

"Dears, dears, let's get moving." Priscilla heightened her interest in the other children, awaiting some sort of instruction, and poked her plump round head outside to face the murky elements. It was quiet, and it was so obvious to William that Priscilla was avoiding his inquisition.

"Priscilla, what happened?"

Priscilla leant close to William, rather too close; she smelt of ash. Her words hissed out. "Dear, what was I thinking inflicting you with magic which clearly lingered? But now, as you seem to know so much, I need my revenge, it's untrue. That's all you need to know."

"Revenge? Against Xavishum? Priscilla, who *are* you really?"

"It seems pretty calm out here now," Angus remarked; thankfully for Priscilla who could now escape William's constant questioning. "The night has passed, and so have those serpents it seems. Safe to get out of here, come on." Angus was the first to heave himself from the cramped hollow tree conditions. "Quite warm, in fact." Angus sounded happy. Quite charming for once.

"I can't quite believe you're actually not moaning!" Belle was the next to scramble up, grabbing at ancient tree roots to aide her. "Thanks," she blushed as Angus held her hand and pulled her up the last steep hillock. "You seem happier now."

"Wouldn't you be if you knew Armageddon was about to be abolished? You weren't about to embark on a life of slavery and debauchment? That you could

171

perhaps, one day, eat white chocolate again? With those little glittery pink sprinkles on top?"

"Well, Angus Moon, I suppose so." Belle stood next to him, her hair completely matted and Angus grinned. "What's so funny?" she flushed.

"Just you, Belle, just you," Angus laughed. "I wouldn't worry. We all love you the way you are."

"The way I am? Idiot."

Alyssa stepped out the hollow in the ground with such pure ease, enhancing Belle's clumsiness. She sighed. Belle rolled her eyes. "I guess we better just keep going, find our way back home." That sounded the most grounded, sensible suggestion, and as William and Priscilla grasped clumps of rock and stone to scrabble from their home inside the old fir tree Priscilla smiled at William.

"It's our secret, dear. Keep our little chat secret…for now. I'll let you know when we need to act," and Priscilla emerged from the hollow quite undisturbed for the sake of the others. "This way, dears, follow me this way. Time to rest before school begins, although the birds are already up in the pond." They were indeed, the day had nearly begun. School was going to be tiresome that day. And for Angus, that Maths test was still chalked up on the board.

Through the Time Travel Tunnel

"Knock knock, William, are you *with* us?" Miss Terrine rapped on the boy's desk. William shot up.

"Yes, absolutely, Miss," William replied, not having heard a single word Miss Terrine had spoken during *'History of Art through the Ages.'* "Great watercolours in that one, I think anyway." William pointed to a random old painted piece hanging from the rafters in the century old built classroom.

"William, you clearly have *not* been listening. We are discussing oil painting techniques, not Alyssa's wishy-washy mindful artwork from last term. Really, do buck up your listening skills and pay attention. Holding your head in your hands with your eyes tight shut will not help your understanding and appreciation of..." but Miss Terrine was cut short as the classroom door flew open.

"Sorry to disturb." Professor Vixonight entered the classroom. "Can I see one of your pupils, Miss Terrine? William Joy, I need your assistance." The Professor nodded his head in William's direction, urging to the tired young boy to exit the classroom. William did look sorrowful that morning. His eyes were as sallow as the setting sun after a storm, and the bags beneath them; sacks of coal. Heavy coal.

"If you must, if you must. Actually, be my guest, William's been nothing more than hopeless today. Let's hope your talk with him will awaken his thoughts somewhat. William Joy, you are just so plainly not going to bed early enough. Belle's the same, she was positively asleep in her rhythmic poetry painting efforts this morning..." but Miss Terrine was cut short yet again as the classroom door shut with a bang, shaking the blackboard of its writing. "Really, that man, he shan't last long around these parts," Miss Terrine uttered and continued her oil painting discussions, creating a faint sprinkle of sparkling black dust which clearly made all the children sit up and listen. Scorchingly intense frowns were forced upon their faces.

Alyssa sat bolt upright. The dust smelt revolting, but no one else seemed to care. She covered her nose. Inhaling the dust had made everyone quite the subservient listener but Alyssa knew better. "Black sorcery. The goblin," she whispered to herself. "Jumping platypus, she's really starting to show her true colours." Alyssa sat still and just stared down trying not to draw attention to her ashen-sickened face. She held her breath. "Just need to go to the toilet, Miss," and before Miss Terrine had time to turn around and display her wicked gnarled lips at the girl, Alyssa had left the room, again the ancient wooden door slamming shut. "Phew, Belle." Alyssa collapsed on William's sister who was simply parading the school corridor.

"What's the matter?" Belle caught her friend clumsily. "Aaah, you're a lump! You look awful. What's up?"

"She's really testing us now!" Alyssa huffed and puffed. She felt completely out of breath, brushing the dust from her clothes. "Miss Terrine, she's just cast some sort of dire attention spell on her entire art class. I joined the class today. Miss Terrine asked me to and now I know why. Everyone is just staring obliviously without any self-control at the blackboard in some sort of trance. It's unbelievable. I've no idea what she's about to do. I excused myself and tried not to breathe in her cocktail of a spell, but I think I inhaled a bit. I feel quite giddy." Alyssa looked back through the little glass slit in the classroom door. The pupils were still silent and appeared to be angelic in their stance. They were all transfixed. Even Sheepish Sharon did not flinch when the most enormous hairy spider crawled up her arm. Its legs were crooked, and each limb seemed to cling on. "They're blind! It's those spiders from the cave again. And they stink. I can smell the stench even through the door."

"Where's William?" Belle pushed passed Alyssa to take a look at the classroom herself. "Horrid." Belle shuddered. "It's abnormal to see such passive behaviour. It's not right. There's no way Slim Jim is just sitting there and not picking his nose or shoving marshmallows up Sharon's skirt." Belle shivered. She looked about nervously. She had the most dreadful feeling that Xavishum was close by. "Where *is* Priscilla? If there was ever a time when I really would like to have her shady, and not always accurate, wand flailing about, it certainly is now." Belle started to panic.

"*What's* going on?" Professor Vixonight strolled down the corridor in his old-fashioned black cape. William walked behind. "Why are you both out here?" He sounded his old grim self again.

"Yes, why *are* you out in the corridor, Belle?" Alyssa had completely forgotten to ask Belle why she too was alone, skipping her Maths class.

"I had a call from my Mum, apparently. I was just on my way to Reception to see what on earth she was worried about this time. Last term she actually came to school with a newly knitted fuchsia scarf and matching hat as she thought it was going to snow. Inside! Really, it was the height of summer! She's soooo embarrassing. Then, as I arrived at the school reception desk, Miss Hill just smirked her reply and said that my Mother was a *"little ahead of herself, daft, having just read the weather forecast for New England, America, where blizzards were starting to cascade."* Anyway, let's hope I'm not about to experience another embarrassing escapade like that. My ego wouldn't be able to cope."

Professor Vixonight gnarled. As the corner tip of his lip curled towards an ever-increasingly pointed ear the corridor had an eerie feeling about it. A dark cloud from outside, stretching wildly over the scraggy oak tree, blew up in a torrent, and a sense of not-so-well being ensued.

"Urrr, why is a darkness looming, Professor?" Belle's face fell abhorrent in white fear.

"Autumn is nearly over and Xavishum knows it." The Professor's growl echoed along the white-washed wall as paintings flapped through the corridor in a

178

sudden indoor breeze. An icy chill filled the air. The school's most ancient fireplace blew an almighty torrent of hail down its chimney and soot shot everywhere.

"It's up my nose! It's sooooo itchy!" William sneezed six times.

"And it's in my ears!" Alyssa screamed and shoved her long fingernails inside her ears to pick out massive lumps of coal.

"I can't see!" Belle coughed, rubbing black dust from her eyes and trying to quickly blink away fragments of burnt kindling. "I really can't even see my hand in front of my face!" Belle sobbed and tried to feel her way towards her brother or even just a classroom door to escape. "William, are you there?"

A loud low recognisable cough and splutter at the far end of the corridor eased Belle, but just a little. "Sis, yes I'm here, but no idea where exactly."

"Pickled eggs, me neither!" A familiar Scottish accent sounded right in Belle's ear. "That head boy, Dick, he came into my classroom and demanded that the headmaster see me at once. No idea why?" Angus spoke out. "A ruffled chap, really. In and out in a dash, he was. Never seen him before. Blithering idiot. Came straight to my desk, he did, and ushered me along just after Belle disappeared. He was an odd sort of boy to be head boy. Careless and not at all polite and commanding like you, Alyssa." Belle rolled her black eyes. It hurt. "I found it all quite strange. It happened far too quickly to recollect. Oh, but Dick, he did have a stick. Whittled if I remember rightly? Head boyhood has gone to his head, for sure."

The black soot cleared a little. It was just enough for the faces in the corridor to make each other out. The smell of charcoaled wood and burning embers lingered, but the air only cleared marginally.

"There is no Dick for head boy in this school," Professor Vixonight replied, glancing around and prowling low. "This year is still under decision. William *was* to be named..."

"Was I? Really?" William looked bashful. "*I* was to be chosen for head boy? But I'm not even in the top class yet."

"You?" Belle threw back her head. "*You?* Head boy? You can hardly get your pants on the right way around, let alone represent the school!"

"You were nominated, by all accounts, last term. Miss Terrine thought you quite the character, I recall. Others agreed, but then you fell from that old oak tree and the offering was put on hold to make sure you had all your wits about you, I heard Mrs Lovett mention. Quite worried they all were. But Terrine? She was sure you were the one. Quite at their wits end with me for being too carefree, they said. Letting you all climb trees. Said I was a danger! But I knew you were fine." The old man bent even lower than Belle had ever noticed before.

"Who called me out here, then? That supposed Dick?" Angus coughed as the fireplace suddenly appeared right by his side. It threw out a disgusting black shot of cinders. Angus sneezed. His whole body shook with cold. The fireplace wood burned a dull red in the grate, but the hollow chimney housed a great icy chill. "Is winter here?" The Scot looked pale. "Well? Has that time finally come?"

"Yes dear, yes dear, but we can't get taken in. We have to prosper. We've come this far." Priscilla shuffled along the corridor, her arms waving through the thick soot to clear a tread-worthy path.

"Priscilla, at last! What's that in your hand?" Belle peered down at Priscilla's black-gloved fingers to catch a greenish sparkle try, not very well, to challenge its beholder. "It looks like a stick, but on the other hand it certainly is the colour and the length of your wand. What's happened to it?"

"Nothing dear, nothing." Priscilla tried to rattle her hands and cover the stick, but the stick definitely remained more stick-like than wand-like.

"Dick! That was the stick Dick was holding!" Angus blurted out. "It most definitely is. I remember that knobbly bit right on the end, can't forget that! It hit me twice swiping me so fast from the classroom my behind cheeks are still pounding; wasn't greatly inspired by fractions, but still, look at the bruises on my knuckles that thing gave me! I was brandished in that classroom. Hastily as anything it whacked me out the door..."

"Alright, alright, I had to make it look authentic, did I not?" Priscilla found she could not make any eye contact with anyone.

"*Were* you Dick, Priscilla? *Were* you?" Belle stared at the witchety-lady. "And my Mum on the telephone? Did you masquerade as her to get me out into the corridor? Did you? I bet you did!"

"Well, I had to get you all out somehow. All of you. This smoky corridor isn't the best, but look in the classrooms." Priscilla tapped her stickety-wand on Miss Terrine's old oak door.

"Blimey! Look! Everyone is still in a trance, but it looks like Miss Terrine is too?" Belle quivered as she glanced every which way. "Isla, Robyn, look, even Timid Trish on the back row! She's so wide-eyed it's untrue. Looks like she's sat on a pin! Did *you* create all this black smoke, Priscilla? It's vile!"

"And it's clogged up my ears, and my nose now!" Alyssa coughed as if the world was about to end.

"Fiddlesticks, don't be so ridiculous! Come on. Follow me. This way. Quick smart." Priscilla ordered. "We can't take the front door. There's a strange pale girl guarding it, very serpent like her features so not the best way out. Come this way..." Priscilla led the team of coughing, spluttering idiots down a narrowly lit, and extraordinarily narrowly built, corridor the pupils had actually never noticed.

"What about the others? We can't leave them with Terrine, that evilton, that goblin might...k...k...kill them all? I'm not keen on maths but I wouldn't go that far! It would be on my conscience forever." Angus kicked the floor.

"She shan't, she shan't..." Priscilla enforced. "She's just Miss Terrine, your art teacher, and Miss Pottage? She's simply maths for you, Angus. Terrine can't kill.

She might be stern, but not that bad." Priscilla bumbled along, shimmering black dust falling from her wand and sending Angus on her tail quite giddy. "I need to get you all out safely now."

"How do you know we need to get out now?" Belle frowned. "And that black dust, shimmering. That's what Miss Terrine used."

"I had to entrance the pupils somehow. I had to cause chaos to be able to escape this place. Spells, smoke, they seemed the answer. Even Terrine got a shot of my *'Make You Enhanced and Blazé Spell.'* Xavishum can't see through smoke. Come *on*, Xavishum's cloud is blowing up thicker and blacker above that old oak tree. It does rumble so." Priscilla floated her way down the thinner and thinner corridor, never ending in length, until at last she forced herself out through a chink of light into the thickest woodland ever. "Phew. It worked. Back to the olden days, but hide, Mother's coming." Priscilla hid behind the thorniest bush and did not budge.

"Your Mother?" Belle enquired. "I really *am* confused. Why is *your* Mother here, Priscilla?"

"Needed to get you out that school, and the only way was this corridor." Priscilla glanced about. "I built it years ago in case I needed to escape one day. Then I set a spell that only I could ever find it and use it to my desire. And it worked!" Priscilla patted herself on the back with her stick; the last of the black shimmering dust falling to the ground and disintegrating into the deep chocolate brown soil.

Angus sat down on a rock. "Don't even try me. Don't even begin to explain anything, Belle. My mind is far too full of what do you call it? Spells and sorcery and plain madness."

"Me too." Belle agreed for the first time. "But don't get involved in a parallel universe, Priscilla. Goodness knows what might become of you and that wand."

Priscilla sniggered. "Don't fret, don't fret. Mother will pass us soon...there. I see quite a lot of that, my own Mother, bless her, when I'm travelling down inside one of my Past Times Tunnels. Ahhh, doesn't she look cute?"

"Cute? *Cute?* Frustrated, I'd say!" Angus shook his head. "Mortified, in fact!"

"Back in the day! It was so funny! Oops, did you see that? An orange hit her square in the face! That was me! Wasn't I bad? I always tried to turn her mad. I used to use my *'Invisible-Invisibah'* tricks on her. See those

185

leaves rustle? That must be me running to hide in case my spell back-fired and I became visible. Blimey, I think it was definitely me who turned her mad."

Angus put his head in his hands. "I should think there's no doubt about that! Heaven's above, and more." He collapsed to the floor.

Priscilla looked excited, fraternising with herself. Her face looked smug and she stood tall (if that was indeed possible.)

"Why were you making time travel pathways?" Belle asked quietly, but Priscilla pretended not to hear. "Priscilla?" Belle did not give up. "Priscilla, I know you can hear me," she said again, moving closer this time.

"Ssh dear. She's coming! Can't have her see me. Now that *would* confuse Mother. She's confused enough without adding to it. Spells have fuzzled her brain and if she saw me, older and wiser than herself, well, let's not think of the consequences that would unravel," Priscilla replied to herself.

"I keep telling everyone not to dabble in parallel universes, but no one seems to listen." Belle sounded so put out. "I'm sure if we continue to flit about we'll only end up lost."

"Belle, just think. If being in Anouka really doesn't change our time at home, and all seems perfectly static, we could stay for a while. See what's here? We'll just come back and sort out our messes later!" Angus's eyes lit up.

"Angus, no! I forbid you to run off and lose yourself. You could easily end up changing life as we know it! We'd probably all turn into chimpanzees. In fact, I know you'd make a complete idiot of yourself, and us. Probably end the world!"

"Cool!"

"I know you are only trying to avoid that maths test. You've been dreading it forever, and you haven't actually been at our school forever so that proves you keep harping on. Is no one sane? Have you all forgotten why we are actually here?" Belle huffed. She felt her blood boil and she shook her head so violently Angus just shrank back.

"Woah! Alright Belle, it was only a thought. I thought we might just find some answers here, that's all." Angus tutted.

"I certainly don't think so! Goodness knows what questions you'd be asking for answers. The answers to Geography tests more like. We need to get back and see if Xavishum is stealing our school, that's what we need to do. Priscilla, the tunnel, we better had get back..." Belle started to turn around to the drainpipe of a hole from which they had appeared, but she stopped dead in her tracks. "What on earth...?" she cried quietly turning pale. "Priscilla?" Belle could only look to the witch for answers. "Priscilla!" Belle quivered. What Belle saw shocked not only herself but the entire group of gawping mouths who simply stuck to the spot.

"I guess I told you we could find some answers here." Angus chuckled.

"Priscilla?" Belle shouted, this time loudly and in control as she saw herself, dressed in her school uniform smiling, but ashen and intense, run past the bush behind which she cowered in secrecy, dropping a trail of rainbow coloured gems. "Priscilla, please? That is me, is it not? Why am I here, and also over there? We've gone back in time not forward, surely? You're a little girl quite plainly by that stream, your Mother ushering you home in fear of some dreadful creature about to pelt her...again! But why am *I* here in parallel?" Belle peered at herself closer. Her school pullover was marked with red paint. "My Mum is a stickler for cleanliness. I've not got dirty all term. I don't remember

188

making my clothes so messy. Priscilla!" Belle became angry as she looked at her happy other-self scatter colourful stones. But she went pale when she saw shadows loom behind her. "Priscilla, there's others after me!" Belle held her breath.

"Dear, dear, don't fuss. You asked if there was anyone sane here. Well, it looks like you are, dear. My time travel tunnels are not quite what I set out to achieve. You see Quindig got in the way, oh yes and my dear dear Myriad. So when I created these time travel tunnels, these havens in which to escape, Quindig and Myriad got between me and my wand, got a taste of the sorcery. I guess that's why they sometimes wake up youthful or rather mature these days, future or past, not quite sure." Priscilla spoke off on a complete tangent. "Heavens, hadn't thought of that?" Belle could see Priscilla frantically nodding her head having answered another one of her many unanswered spell misdemeanors. "Anyway, anyway, I created little escape hatchways and pathways as go-betweens in and out of Anouka and your time, to help, to look forward, to look back, to succeed, to defeat Xavishum, and you see, now you are privy to this, we can achieve all sorts together. I had to plan from when I was only a girl. I always knew. Quindig never believed me when I said atrocities would occur. He thinks I'm a mad old bat! But I *always* knew." Priscilla whispered this last part in just Belle's listening ear. Belle frowned. She trusted this bad mad witch, and as she glanced up, her messy clothed-self had vanished leaving only a long line of turquoise-red gem stones paving the way forward.

"How will I know to come and leave those?" Belle whispered back to Priscilla, but the mad sorceress was already deep into the forest following each individual gem.

William was the last to gather his thoughts and head into the thicket of a wood. He looked back as he stepped forward and frowned. Listening hard, pressing his left ear up against an array of thorns which covered the clever little tunnel from which they had emerged, William could hear whispering. At first, the whispers were non-intelligible, but as his ears got accustomed to the tone he realised what he could hear was the same twisted serpents' voices from before. The words the serpents' spoke came thick and fast. William had to listen intently to catch it all.

"She went down here, the goblin went down here," the master's voice hissed. "Xavishum must know of this. The goblin did not mention her intent to exit the school today, the agenda was to stay with the guardsssssssssssss on the gate and collect those four children. Sssssss. Maybe the goblin has a different agenda?"

William's eyes widened and he jumped back. "My God!" He cried in fear. "Priscilla, the goblin followed us down here. I understood the master serpent tell us so." Standing around was not in William's best interests, hovering at the end of the tunnel where the goblin was surely soon to appear, and the boy shot off to find his companions. "Priscilla!" William cried once more, masterfully this time. "I think we'd better make ourselves scarce as any minute the goblin will be upon us." William finally, breathless, caught up and tugged Priscilla's chiffon layers. "Got another spell ready yet, another time travel tunnel?" William puffed. "Because if there is a time to make one happen, now would be it, and I do mean right NOW! Xavishum's goblin…is…right…behind…us." He gabbled out his words so fast his tongue became twisted.

"What?" Angus jittered on the spot. "I've surely had enough for today. That maths test seems a breeze. Bring it on please, Miss Pottage. Honestly, I'm wretched with all this serpent stuff." But Angus ran just like the others. He did not look back.

"Duck! There's your Mother again!" Belle cried in her loudest whisper.

"Thank you, dear. Much obliged." Priscilla appeared unperturbed. "Mother, oh you always were such a skittish lady." Priscilla was quite calm given their predicament. "Just here, Belle's gems turn this corner, just here. Great. I could never have remembered the way to the tunnel's other exit without your help, Belle." Priscilla nodded towards the running female.

"But I still don't understand," Belle shouted, breathless, and looked at her trail of glittering colourful gems behind them through the vast thick trees. "How will I know when to come? To escape that goblin on our trail I'll need to have laid all of those." Belle pointed back to her mingled bright pathway. "If I don't come, we'll be lost...and be that goblin's prey for sure." A tear crept into Belle's eye and her worried expression poured a grey hue onto her cheeks.

"Dear, dear, you'll know," Priscilla whispered. "You came, didn't you?"

Gemstone Delights?

It was dark as William and Belle trudged home. Very dark. Past the lifeless pond onto which the full moon beamed its silvery rays. Across the road where the mirrored wall had once tricked them, Belle lumbered along, slowing at each step until she nearly stopped altogether.

"I'm exhausted," Belle admitted to herself.

"And *I* am to be head boy," William replied back.

"Is that *all* you can say?" Belle's pace got slower and slower until William had to physically drag his sister up the steep cottage steps home. "Goodness knows what Mum will say when she sees those red-stains all over my school pullover."

"Belle, is that all *you* can say?" William laughed in jest. "Anyway, that sketch hasn't even happened yet."

The cottage stable door flew open and a gregarious plume of bitter-smelling black smoke billowed outside, followed by great guffaws and a charcoal-faced coughing woman. William ran up.

"Mum! Are you okay?" William suddenly knew exactly how Myriad must feel every day. Priscilla was his own Mum's sorcerer equivalent. His Mother, the terrible culinary novice, and Priscilla? - their not so gracious witch.

"Don't mind me, don't you mind me. You carry on," Mrs Joy replied, choking and spluttering within the grey cloud of smoke which appeared to be following her everywhere. "I'm trying a new recipe. *Gemstone Delights* at apparently six o'clock precisely. Your new cookery teacher, preposterous in her demands, called quite out the blue and threw my schedule simply out of the window. Didn't have half the ingredients but, what was her name, it's slipped right out my mind, anyway, the school needed an exact recipe for tomorrow's *Teacher of the Term* election, and...Miss *Pree* Cilla, that's it, I remember now, well, she thought of me and my delightful biscuits of late and asked if I was at all flexible in what I could bake? Well, of course I obliged but, Belle, this is my third batch already. The gemstone biscuits, tiny as they may be, just keep exploding. I have no idea what I am doing wrong?"

"Oh," Belle remarked, and she picked up her Mother's hand written scrawl of a recipe. "Are you adding the correct amount of blue, green and red food colouring? We did some odd experiment in Chemistry last term, and if the quantities of any solution were just fractionally out then, well, poor Scrawny Simon's petri-dish just flew up to the classroom ceiling. It took ages for our aged-old caretaker to scrape the mess off the walls." Belle bent down and peered inside the oven. Batch four appeared to be bubbling away nicely. "These look okay, Mum. Nearly done, I think." Belle pulled down the cast iron door handle, the glass front opening slowly forward.

"Belle, no, they always look perfect until minute eleven on the timer, then..." Belle's Mum voiced her knowledge but it was just too late. *BANG!*

"Oh, ouch, that's hot!" Belle jumped back from the Aga as thirty six Gemstone Delights exploded their entire insides onto Belle's school uniform. "It's ruined, sorry Mum." Belle stared in horror at her crusty wet red-stained pullover.

"Belle, Belle, entirely my fault. I shouldn't have involved you in my more delicate baking requests. There's the new cleaning lady arriving tomorrow night. Can that pullover do just one more day, dear? I'll write the school a note." Belle's Mum looked in desperation at her ghastly gemstone attempts. They were far from Gemstone Delights as required.

"Perhaps leave them baking for twelve minutes, the next batch?" and William glared at his sister to follow him upstairs, leaving their hot and bothered Mother to clean up and try again.

William and Belle looked as thick as thieves taking the staircase three steps at a time. "Crazy!" William cried as they slammed their bedroom door. "Priscilla's even got Mum on the case baking for some sort of event! Those Gemstone Delights, if they work, are your jewels for the path you lay in Priscilla's time travel tunnel, for sure. And your pullover? Well that's to be scrubbed as good as new after this day, so I guess there's your answer. I heard you ask Priscilla. It's tomorrow you lay your path."

"Yes." Belle didn't sound so sure.

"What's up? Seamless to me." William frowned at Belle. She appeared distraught.

"It's not that. I suppose I know I *must* play the game tomorrow," she muttered. "But how do I know when exactly, or even where to go?"

William slapped her on the shoulder. "Get in there girl! Come on! Priscilla won't leave you in the lurch, Belle. Come on, get with it. Priscilla will know. Wait until tomorrow, you'll see. I'm sure we'll all soon see."

And, unlike William, he opened his English prose and wrote an essay like he had never written before.

"Must be Priscilla's magic still lingering," Belle yawned, watching her brother's concentration to literacy detail far too spot on. But she could not quite keep her eyes open to see William finish.

***

Mrs Joy sat in her kitchen rocking backwards and forwards in her old creaky chair. Her brow was now dripping with perspiration. Her pinny was ruined but at least she had a beautiful array of thirty six Gemstone Delights sat on the worktops. Still encased in their baking trays she re-read the scrawl she had taken from Pree Cilla and realised if she had only taken a few more moments to digest the baking method properly she would have seen she had indeed written *'bake for twelve minutes exactly, not more and absolutely not less, for fear of dire consequences.'*

"Dear, dear," Mrs Joy muttered to herself. "More haste, less speed, I really should follow my own advice by admittance," and she continued to rock backwards and forwards before realising it was pitch black outside and she had not heard a peep from William and Belle for hours. "Heavens and treacles, I did not feed my babies! Obsessed with these here Gemstone Delights and not a care for anyone else." She crept upstairs.

As Mrs Joy neared the second staircase which lead to the attic room it was still so incredibly silent she dare not enter for fear of disturbing the peace, but she could not resist just a little peek. The pine door creaked. Stair nine creaked as normal. Mrs Joy continued up to the top stair. All was still blissfully silent, and she was just about to head back down and turn her mind to cooking a Fisherman's Gratification for Mr Joy when a light through the partially drawn curtains caught her eye. She crept over to the window and squinted through the condensation on each sash pane trying to fathom out the odd glow, in fact two small odd glows, bright fiery orange flicking glows in the distance. "Strange?" Mrs Joy whispered aloud. She could not figure them out and there was certainly no street light quite there; the council would never stump up extra money to light more than two places in the village, and they were the local pubs. Funny that, she had always thought. Mrs Joy squinted further, pressing her nose up to the wet panes of glass. "How odd. Those two bright lights are in the middle of a corn field."

Mrs Joy muttered to herself some oddities which even she did not quite understand so how they could be described would be a mystery, but she squinted more to focus better. "What are they? What can possibly be sitting in a corn field at this time of night? Looks like a pair of animal eyes, but far, far too large for a cat or even a fox." Mrs Joy blinked, but when she looked back outside the orange lights were gone.

"Mum? Mother, what *are* you doing?" William had woken up. "What's out there?" he whispered across the room before placing both of his feet out from beneath his bed covers and tiptoeing to the sash windows to take a look for himself.

"Oh William, don't shake yourself from your dreams, dear. I've been far too long glaring into my dimly lit Aga I'm actually seeing its fiery warmth out there. Spots of bright orange on the field horizon before my very eyes just like the glow from the oven. Tiredness, I expect. Gemstone Delight explosions in my face, something like that! Hop back into bed, come on." And the delirious woman motioned William back under his heated quilt before she too headed to bed. "Night, William," she whispered.

"Oh, yes, night," William replied. He waited. "Weirdo." And he crept back to the sash window as soon as he heard his bedroom door shut tight. "Or is she?" From beneath his attic room William heard a muttering and a loud rustle. He laughed. *"What am I doing going straight to bed? I should be cooking mild-green pea-ish soup with zesty orange rind for tea."* William listened to his Mother's astounded realisation. "Yep, she is."

Glancing through the sash window, dripping with night dew, William saw nothing at first. He moved his eyes every which way from farmers' corn fields to his neighbouring garden lawn. It was kept, devastatingly to Mr Joy, clipped and sheared to less than one millimetre of its life.

"Not much growth for imagination there," William's Father had been heard saying. *"Where will the spring ducklings hatch in such clear conditions? Need foliage and wild bullrushes if you want to attract nature."* Not everyone wanted a nature reserve on their doorstep William used to jeer. *"Well, they should."* And that would be that.

William yawned. He continued to peer into the late darkness of the sky. "Huh?" He jumped back. There were not two small fiery orange lights on the horizon now but two enormous fiery orange lights staring right back at him through the window pane not a centimetre from his nose .He could not work it out. William reached for his fountain pen, for some strange reason, and heralded it out forwards towards the luminous dazzling lights. His eyes widened and a rap on the glass from a large sharp white claw caused him to gasp out loud. *"Blimey!"* He shrieked.

"What? Sorry? William? What *is* it? Is it the goblin?" Belle shot up in her bed. "Well? William?"

William cast the blue ink from his weapon at the beast and Belle gasped. "What on earth are you doing? That's going to stain the carpet! Are you mad? William, are you sleep-walking?" Belle cried as loudly as she dared.

"I don't know! I don't know *what* I'm doing. It just jumped up at me, my pen!" William looked at his hands covered in ink. It dripped onto the floor and down the walls. "Oops!" Then he got the shock of his life. "Belle! Rosabella! What is *THAT?*"

Belle ran across the room, slipping on the inky carpet. "What *is* that?" She reached out her puny fingers, only the thin glass separating her from some beast. She ran her fingernails down the cold panes. "Woah. Look at this, orange fiery eyes, scathing claws, jees, it's back!" William flicked more of what seemed poisonous ink at the intruder.

"William!" Belle squinted. "William, it's Vixonight! Let him in!" And Belle, still dressed in her stained school pullover, wrenched the ancient sash window open. It graunched under its own pressure. Vixonight swiftly pounced inside.

"Thank you," he growled, licking a fresh wound on his hind paw. "Thank you. I need shelter, my home, it's dishevelled, ransacked. I can't stay there anymore. *She's* found me."

"You want to stay here?" William cried.

"Of course he does." Belle stroked the beast's bleeding limb. It dripped onto the carpet.

"For now, I will," Vixonight demanded, allowing no further room for debate.

"Okay." William nodded. "Take my bed." William pointed to his, rather small for a grown werewolf, bed for the night. Professor Vixonight laughed.

"It's not such a silly idea." William looked annoyed. He had given up his bed after all. "You'll be changing back into your smaller human self soon and it will be just fine." But the beast was asleep on the hearth by the disused fireplace grate. "Oh. As you wish." William crept back to sleep.

The Open Grate

A small chink of light fell upon the attic room carpet. A new day had begun. William woke with a start. "Professor?" he whispered quietly. "Professor Vixonight?" William sat up. He rubbed his eyes and blinked. The hearth grate lay cold and the rug at its feet lay empty. "Professor? Where are you?" William jumped up, pushing an enormous hefty black book to the floor. It landed on its spine with a thud, the clatter disturbing Belle.

"Professor Vixonight?" Belle called out. As she looked towards the thick woven rug she also realised it lay alone. Just a few drops of deep red blood left behind. "Where's the Professor? William, he's disappeared."

The ancient sash windows sat firmly closed. The crimson quilted curtains drawn shut, just their normal line of sunshine peeping through. Mrs Joy had embroidered the curtains years ago, but had measured the panes ever so hastily, and for as long as William and Belle could remember, the hanging curtains had been ill-fitting.

"William, he's gone, and it wasn't a dream. I did let the Professor in last night. Didn't I? Look, your blue ink stain's everywhere, and the Professor's blood has dripped all over the hearth. But William, he can't have walked downstairs to get out, the droplets of blood are only here. How can he have just vanished? What's that book?" Belle stretched and walked over to sit on William's mattress, still trying to figure out how the Professor had left their bedroom.

William picked up the old-looking large leather bound book. "I don't know where it came from, or what it is really."

"Is it your English Prose?" Belle elbowed William. "Well? Get all your homework done now. Perhaps you're still dosed-up with Priscilla's magic? You not only wrote a masterpiece but you bound it as well!"

Mr Joy called from the ground floor kitchen. "Rancid porridge ready for the taking, slurp it if you dare!" William and Belle heard him chuckle. "The Joy Woman has certainly outdone herself this time with the likes of cookery. Heaven knows what these hard shiny balls are in their baking cases. Apparently an offering for *Teacher of the Term* this morning, but unless she plans to break some teeth along the way, they're a bit over-done. Oh, I only said *a bit*." Mrs Joy must have come in.

"The Gemstone Delights. *Your* Gemstone Delights." William grabbed Belle's arm and, temporarily forgetting about the disappearance of Professor Vixonight, Belle was pulled, two stairs at a time, down to the kitchen. William had the book tucked under his arm, not noticing one page floating on its own by a large white feather. It marked a chapter.

"Where's Mum gone now? She's never out the door this early." Belle moved her spoon about in her bowl. Rancid milk slopped over the side.

"Gone to meet Prissy." Mr Joy stayed in the kitchen. His arms appeared to be stuck in the sink. "These rubber gloves. Never again will I wear these. My hands have turned pink." He continued to mumble. Suds slopped onto the floor.

"Prissy, who's Prissy?" William joined in. He was suspicious of everyone nowadays.

"Prissy? She's our new cleaning lady. Arrives today. Great references. She could even sponge werewolf's blood from an old carpet, her last employer said. Great recommendation if ever I heard one," Mr Joy whispered. "More porridge?" He continued to ladle out two ongoing bowls of milky soup into new bowls. "Enough?" and he strode back into the kitchen. "What is it with you?" Mr Joy shook his head as both idle children slopped their entire porridge contents onto the carpet. "You both quite alright?" William and Belle choked. "I told your Mother that porridge of hers would kill someone one day."

Belle leant across the table. "It's Priscilla, isn't it? It has to be. Coming to live at our house! Blimey." And not knowing what else to say, she tucked into her drinkable breakfast, the inch that was left at the bottom of the bowl.

***

William slurped his spoon. Then he remembered the book. "Oh," and he pulled it from beneath his baggy jumper. The book fell open at the marked page, and the pure white feather fell to the floor. As it fluttered, William read. The chapter was entitled *'Time Travel Tunnels Least Expected.'* "Belle, this book's been marked. It's fallen open just here. For you." William twisted the heavy book onto its spine towards his sister, and as she drank the last remnants of her porridge she cast her eyes upon the book's words. It was poetry.

'Where you follow your dream is just your haven
But make sure you look.
Right beside the warming fire is the path I took.'

"Strange." Belle squinted. "Sounds more like some sort of puzzle. Anyway, where did you get this book, William?"

"From nowhere, I just found it lying on my bed this morning. That was the clatter."

Belle glanced back at the verse she had just read. "Dreams?" she whispered. "William, this verse talks about dreams, here look." And she read the verse quietly again.

'Where you follow your dream is just your haven
But make sure you look.
Right beside the warming fire is the path I took.'

"William, I think the verse is talking about our bedroom. Weird! *Our* bedroom? That's a bit close for comfort." Belle continued to whisper. "There must be something in our bedroom..." She shivered. "*Hey!*" Belle jumped back in her chair. A soft prickle had brushed past her bare leg. She looked underneath the table. "Naribu!" Belle exclaimed. The white feather had changed into Naribu. He fluttered out from beneath the wooden table legs and perched on the back of Belle's chair. "What are *you* doing here?"

"Well that's no welcome for a long lost friend! How about a bit of *"Nice to see you!"* the old owl remarked. "I needed to mark the page." Naribu preened his other shimmering feathers; the ones which were actually still attached to his body. "Dear, dear, deary me. Poor Vixonight was close to death last night," Naribu turned his voice to the most serious lurid tone Belle had ever heard. "I realised from afar he had not marked the page of this book. Xavishum turned his house upside down looking for it. There's a written chapter on *'How To Slay Krook, And Lock It Back Up Like Before.'* She needed to take this book, delete it from history before Vixonight found that chapter and imprisoned her and her fiends for eternity. Vixonight's been searching for the chapter for *years*. But still not found it. Look how long the book is." Naribu's beak flicked through the chapters. As he did so the book never got shorter, in fact it grew in length twice as fast as the wise old owl could even turn each page.

"That's incredible!" William remarked, astonished. "Incredible. How does it do that?"

"Every witch or wizard in the land can write spells, verse, even cryptic clues and add them to this book. It's *'The Sorceror's Encyclopedia.'* This Encyclopedia is so magic one does not even need to be in possession of it to add ideas. Knowledge is evolving all the time." Naribu preened his pure white plumage to an inch of its life.

"I did wonder why it was getting heavier and heavier just in the space of time it took me to get downstairs." William still looked amazed. "Does it do my homework?"

"William!" Belle hit him.

"What's going on in there?" Mr Joy was still fighting with his ridiculous gloves.

"I think we need to find another tunnel." Belle shuddered. "I hate tunnels."

Naribu blinked in his own confident way and began to appear quite old and quite translucent. He swept lowly up the staircase so quietly and so swiftly the children had to follow his trail quite fast, tumbling over their school bags en route. Mr Joy called up after them. "It's time to leave. The school bell will be ringing in eleven minutes." But even Belle's appetite for promptness was not enough. She dashed up the last of the steps into their attic room, and was just timely enough to see Naribu vanish into the cold disused fire grate.

"He went in there, inside our fireplace," Belle cried breathlessly. "That must be the tunnel Vixonight is referring to." *'Right beside the warming fire is the path I took.'*

It was not very often that Mr Joy hurried along the children on a school day, and today he had been left solely in charge. He heard a series of whispering tones and followed William and Belle up to their attic room to catch their conversation from the bottom attic step.

"He went in there! A smidgen of dust mingled with the air as I crashed into our room and then the owl disappeared." Mr Joy overheard Belle.

"It's a sign! Vixonight must have left our house by that fire grate opening whilst we were sleeping, and sure enough Naribu has now shown us the way. It must be another of Priscilla's time travel tunnels. That's a turn up for the books." Mr Joy listened intently, frowning, and he ascended to the top. Step nine creaked on his approach, luckily obscuring William's next words.

"Anouka's now in our home. Must always have been...oh, Dad. How long have you been there?" William shot a desperate glance at his sister, whilst familiar voiced whisperings came from within their fireplace. One voice sounded like Belle, getting louder and laughing, and sounding completely elated. William picked up a large round pebble and threw it directly into the grate. It clattered inside and the voices, once quite loud, came to an abrupt halt, followed by peace.

"What's going on? William, why did you throw that enormous pebble in there? It'll break the fireplace. Do you know how old these things actually are?" Mr Joy sounded annoyed, most out of character for him, but luckily questions were saved by Mrs Joy and Pree Cilla's heads appearing.

"William? Rosabella? Why are you still at home? Really Nicholas..." she turned to her husband. "You only had to get them out the house. Breakfast was already laid on."

"Yes, we know," Belle replied, rolling her eyes and making gagging sounds.

"Aww, thanks dear," Mrs Joy smiled at her daughter.

"No worries." Belle still had her fingers part way down her throat.

"Those Gemstone Delights only had to be boxed up. It was not too much of a hardship. Chop chop..." and Mrs Joy ushered the children past Pree Cilla.

"You might as well meet Prissy on the way. She's come to...oh, make a start on your bedroom. I can see the carpets are terrible! What on earth happened? I must be day-dreaming half of the time. I hadn't at all noticed they were indeed so filthy. Sorry Prissy." Mrs Joy cast a half ashamed face in Pree Cilla's direction.

"Hello!" Belle beamed as she passed the cleaning lady on the stairs. "I'm Belle, and this is William. Gracious, Pree Cilla, what on earth have you done to your forehead?" Belle pointed to a rather nasty bruise growing bigger and bigger into a large crimson bump just above Pree Cilla's left eye.

"Prissy, *do* call me Prissy." Priscilla's eyes widened. "Yes, I was struck by a rather unexpected pebble, just flew through the air quite by chance!" she continued, and glared at William.

"Sorry to hear that," William whispered.

"Don't be, don't be, you weren't there...yet," Priscilla whispered into the boy's ear. "Anyway, I'll get on with these stains." Prissy winked and tied her, rather garishly yellow, hair cloth tighter. "Can't let evil filth win," she muttered, glancing into the grate. "It looks like it needs a good clean right inside this old filthy place too. I'll get on with that."

The children pattered downstairs in single file, lost for words. "She's trying to get into the tunnel, clever old thing," whispered Belle into her brother's ear. "She built the tunnel and I expect she knows it comes out in our bedroom, whether she found that out in the past or in the future beats me, but she knows the way."

"Probably meet herself in there again." William shook his head. "Can you imagine Angus trying to fathom all this out? He's a day-by-day chancer, none of this cross-over-in life, it *'fuggles'* his brain, apparently, as he likes to say," and William threw his Mother's, very solid and compressed Gemstone Delights into a fanciful tissue box and shut the stable door behind them trying himself not to frown at the prospect that they had indeed already followed Belle's scattered gemstone path the previous day. It was not only Angus; being a simpleton was just plain easier. "And I still wish that book could do our homework."

Teacher of the Term Unleashed

"Just on here. Lay your offerings just on this table, please. *Matilda!* Don't push! Poor Mrs Lovett is trying her best to make enough room for all of your goodies. My, there has been some tremendous baking going on in your parents' kitchens." Professor Vixonight nodded at William as he placed Mrs Joy's crinkled green covered tissue box with the other culinary delights. "Let's put this one at the front, shall we?" The Professor tried to keep calm and not harbour any preferences, but William could so easily tell that his Gemstone Delights were really, despite sore to the eye, a rare commodity on the table. William bowed his head. They looked awful. Embarrassing wasn't the word. So, he just took his seat with the elder boys at the back of the assembly hall and tried to keep low. His knees knocked.

Spotty Patrick just eyed William up then down. "Weirdo," Patrick mumbled, and shuffled his chair a little further away. His chair legs scraped across the floor.

"WHO is making that dreadful noise?" Professor Vixonight growled from the front of the hall. "Well?" No one owned up. The Professor's hands were pressed firmly into his ears. "Well, *don't* be making it again." His fiery eyes scanned the hall. His nose twitched. "You have been warned."

Patrick just stared at the floor. William smirked.

Professor Vixonight cleared his throat. It was the longest, gravelliest clearing of a throat and none of the pupils knew where to look. He began. "Being new to this school, I thought that I might enlighten you with the type of congratulatory gift I used to excel in passing to the most enlightening teacher at my previous..." Professor Vixonight shuffled on the spot, "...dwelling." He coughed and reached for his water. After an extraordinary long guzzle and a rather gregarious slurping from the jug itself which was rather uncouth, the Professor continued. "This term I am sure that there are a number of pupils who have given great commendation to a number of teachers, and I am sure all the teaching staff's work at this establishment has not gone unnoticed. That, I can assure you all." The Professor looked on edge, and William noticed he did not take his orange eyes off their Mother's box. The box started to show a sign of pale blue smoke, and the lid wobbled up and down quite simply by itself.

As the Professor continued his speech, a low toned rumbling came from the table of offerings, and the Professor threw his black cape across the stage to cover the tremors. "My, there must be some worthy eateries on the table to be letting their boxes move so." All the children covered their faces and William and Belle tried to find each other amongst the crowds in the hall. Their eyes shot in every direction.

"What is *that*?" Matilda cried, pointing to the box right at the front of the table. It was Mrs Joy's Gemstone Delights, and they were causing the table on which they stood, and the floor beneath the table's legs, to shiver and quake, but the green-tissued box remained absolutely still, only a crack of an opening in its lid hissing smoke, deeper and darker in colour. The Gemstone Delights were now rock solid and were not going anywhere, but all the other boxes on the table rattled and eventually fell to the floor; cream and jam sponge flooding the entire front row.

"My tights! My favourite knitted tights!" one stupid girl screamed.

"Mmm, yummy vanilla cream." Glutonous Glenda smacked her fat lips.

"Heavens!" Mrs Lovett cried. She tried to mop up the splattering of dessert which covered the uneven-surfaced ground, but the Professor did not fuss. He kept his eyes still steadily on the green-tissued box, and as William squinted, he could lip read Vixonight's voice as he read a chapter from the *Sorceror's Encyclopedia* whipped from beneath his cloak. That encyclopedia seemed to get everywhere.

"Rise and challenge, travel free, rocks feel desire and worship me.

Your solid mass, your knowledge be, let Belle place you, she'll soon see.

*Then dear sister, you will **die,** your squalid life, will not survive.*

Your aged power will not revive, when you are dead and no longer alive."

William stepped backwards. "Woah! Freaky!" he whispered. He could not believe what he was seeing as Professor Vixonight's lips carefully formed the powerful words of this chapter. But he knew that despite Xavishum being his own flesh and blood, she had to be disempowered for Greer to be free of that wolf-beast who controlled him. William's hearing was heightened so much his ears rang. "Ouch!" He tried to cover the holes in his ears and crouch down to the floor, but the ringing just followed him. It was inside his head. He caught eye contact with the Professor, and as the Gemstone Delights continued to rock and sway alone in their box on the table, the Professor's orange fiery eyes turned to dust, mystifying any pupil or teacher by his gaze.

William looked around. "Blimey!" He called out to his sister. She was not at all mystified, and neither were Angus nor Alyssa. "Belle, grab them!" William cried as his Mother's Gemstone Delights exploded into the air; the rock-type pellets fired high towards the flint built ceiling. Some of them shot right through allowing freezing air to turn William's fingers, and hair, to ice as he reached up.

Belle held out her school book bag as far as she could as a huge amount of rainbow-infused stones tumbled back down her way, but she dropped her catch when it became too heavy. "Flumux-sticks!" she cried. The Professor pushed the encyclopedia back beneath his cloak. William looked towards Angus.

"Don't ask me!" the Scottish boy replied just shaking his head in vain. "I have no idea, but it's a pretty good

God damn show! Follow Belle, she seems to have some sort of clue." Sure enough Belle was clutching as many of the gems as possible and running in through an oak door, an oak door that William had never noticed before. They all dived in behind.

"Not my idea of winning a prize," Angus mumbled, quite upset that he had not seen his favourite tennis coach win all of the cakes and share them with his team. "Thought something weird might happen at this event. Never heard of the like before. Mind you, I thought it was because in Scotland we don't share cakes, share anything come to think of it, and we certainly don't pat people on the back for the best performance."

"This has *never* been here before, in our school," William shouted back, hurriedly traipsing inside the wooden hollow and through the newly created door to where the gemstones were pulling Belle. "Never!"

"Well, perhaps you have never looked hard enough, William." Priscilla's voice appeared to follow him further into the wooded abyss, but the boy could not see her.

"Professor Vixonight, why are we here? Why do I need to lay these gems?" Belle asked the Professor, but as she caught his eye, his demeanour grew stronger and in control.

"Not now." He growled. "Soon." He continued to scour the *Sorceror's Encyclopedia* muttering "Where is that clearing? For Heaven's sake! It *has* to be here, the book says it has to be here." The Professor searched about, he sounded angry, no, he sounded knowledgeable, and so ready for something quite soon.

Belle picked up her book bag. She took a look inside. The stones were indeed gems, and they were glowing very brightly. Just as she put her hand inside, the first gem flew up into her fingers and controlled the configuration of where it should lie. "Oh!" she uttered to herself. "I see." Each gem worked its presence into her grasp and pulled her arm to the forest floor. Belle laughed, she was fascinated with the guidance, and the warmth of the gems made her quite giddy with excitement.

"Is she quite alright?" Angus looked closer. "She's gone a bit, well, funny?"

Belle laughed louder and louder and became quite out of control. As she skipped along an un-predetermined wooded pathway and the gems lay themselves out plain as day, she seemed to be flying behind them.

"Huh?" Angus squinted. "Her feet? Belle's feet, they're not actually touching the floor!" He scratched his head.

"This is marvellous!" Belle was quite delighted but her legs had to move fast to keep up with the gems displacement. William, Angus and Alyssa followed in her path, but kept to the forest walls in each other's shadows. Angus kept to the back.

"Are you scaaaaaaared?" William mocked. "Ha ha, Angus is scared!"

"Not!" Angus flicked his hair.

"Are!" William kicked the floor. Dust flew up. He coughed. Dramatically.

"Sucker!" Angus replied. "Who's scared now?"

"It was just a cough," William spat back.

Priscilla laughed beneath her clothes.

Belle looked ahead. She suddenly became cautious. Her footsteps halted. Her laughter diminished to nothing. She could hear voices and she looked down an alternative path which crossed her. She turned pale. "It's me." Belle quivered. "Blimey, I mustn't see myself and catch my own stare." She ran on as fast as the gems allowed but kept her eyes focused forward. She remembered; she had looked just like that when she had seen herself here before. "Weirder and weirder." Belle muttered.

At a cross in the forest, Belle stopped. She could see a chink of light to her right and a clearing in the forest further into the distance. Her palms started to burn and Belle could feel the gemstones rock around. "They're unsure which path to take, quite unsure," Belle whispered under her breath. She looked towards the light and then spun around to see the dry open space, cleared of twigs and debris, further ahead. "Where are you destined?" She leant towards her open palms as the gemstones flashed hot, creating sparks. "Where do you need to go? Well? Tell me?" she whispered again. The gemstones still just wriggled as if the crossroads in the woods had thrown a curve ball of confusion. "The clearing?" Belle suddenly realised. "Professor Vixonight had muttered something about a clearing, but maybe we're not supposed to go there quite yet, not quite yet?" She looked again towards the dusty area. It was vaguely familiar, with the old oak tree rising from behind. "The old oak tree! Huh, we're back at school! But it all looks so dark and creepy and simply horrid.

And, oh, there are figures, gaunt dark figures cowering by its trunk. Angus? It's Angus, well, a face like Angus but smaller and shallow and somehow elfin like as if he has been left behind to rot in a decrepit dark Anouka. Oh, and the werewolf. Oh Professor, you're so gaunt and emaciated by Angus's side." Belle scratched her forehead. Then a horrible sense of cold realisation crept into her thoughts. "Oh my goodness!" The worst thought struck her. "Heavens! It's the future. It's what this place looks like once Xavishum has won. Bitter and raw, cold and dark and, oh I can't bear to think about how awful it might be." Belle forced to place the gemstones towards the chink of light, turning back to see if anyone was yet with her. A faint flowery pattern appeared through the light. "My wallpaper," she whispered, and the companions on her trail came into view, voicing quite nervous tones at the thought of being lost in the forest.

A loud rustling crack sounded from the thicket of deep green trees above, and just as Belle lay her last gem by the growing chink of light, Priscilla fell from a gorse of prickly leaves.

"Finally! What was all that dilly-dallying about, child?" Priscilla faffed about, pressing her clothes and brushing prickles from her skin. "Goodness me."

"Sorry? Haven't I just saved us?" Belle retorted, really annoyed.

"Yes, yes! Good work, Belle." Priscilla cowered, slightly embarrassed. She walked, quite strangely, looking around. "I just thought you were *never* going to let go of those gemstones. This, this scenario, it's been in the planning for years, with no one believing it to happen, and I thought, well, never mind what I thought, but you've done it now." And, as if in anticipation, she led Belle towards the brightening opening, a tremendous greying rock tumbling from a height striking Priscilla clean on the head. "Yes, yes, I was prepared, as much as can be, but it still hurts regardless," and she collected the companions, one by one, ushering them back into the bedroom.

"Oh, can I sleep with you? There seems to be a lack of beds?" But Angus's remark led to the second bump on the head for the night.

"Of course not, cretin," Belle smirked.

Night fell, clear but overbearing. "Thank you for helping me find one of my time travel tunnels, quite forgetful sometimes, I am. Quick, watch yourselves, you'll be coming through here again in a minute." Priscilla waved her arms. Angus fainted. "See? Well planned, well planned. He doesn't need a bed after all."

Verona's Winter Meets her Match

William sat on his bed staring into the fireplace grate as if searching for a definitive answer, a realisation, when Belle appeared quietly from downstairs.

"Penny for your thoughts?" She prodded her brother. "What is it?"

"How will we know when we are needed, you know? Really needed." William asked.

"Come on! Get with it!" Belle prodded him again. "That's what you said to me!"

"Get lost." William shrugged.

"You mean the exact moment we have to defeat Xavishum?" Belle felt a little mean.

"Yes." William's tone was a worried one. "I know Vixonight has the *Sorceror's Encyclodepia* but he's forever fumbling through chapter-upon-chapter; it will be a miracle if he ever finds exactly what he needs at the right moment, don't you think?"

"Well, I think we just need to have some faith? Some conviction." Belle slumped down onto her bed. "Things do seem to just slot into place. I mean, Priscilla wheedling her way into our house to make use of her time travel tunnel. And Naribu? Just appearing like that.

As for Angus, he's just there. Gets me so hot headed at times, but his effect, well, it just makes me more determined to persevere."

"And you fancy him," William sniggered into his jumper.

"Take that back! I do *not!*" Belle turned her back.

"That's rather philosophical anyway, Belle, but sort of true, I suppose. Still not convinced though." William twiddled his thumbs.

"William, Rosabeeeeeela?" A loud ringing voice reverberated up the stairs. "Angus is here, brought his sledge with him. It's suddenly started to snow, falling quite fast just completely out of the blue, no warning, but makes for a fun afternoon on the hills? Wiiiiiiiiiiiiiiilliam, Belle, can you hear me?"

William and Belle were standing by their sash window. The walk back from school had been quite scorching. The sun had been far too bright white for days now. "Bit weird." Belle frowned, still not forgiving William's outburst about her and Angus.

"Xavishum. This is her doing. It's coming." William shuddered. Belle had kept her vision of the harsh cold winter school at the crossroads in the time travel tunnel, with its crumbling walls and sharp pointed icicles, to herself. She had not told a soul. Something inside her had told her to wait. It was like knowing what the future held was to be her secret. Knowledge only for her. The more she mulled over this concept in her mind, the more she thought about Xavishum. No one, Priscilla, Professor Vixonight, Myriad ever talked about the defeat, they had separate thoughts and never seemed to share the next step as to when or how or even if the light or the dark side were to triumph. It was like each individual had their own agenda, their own reason to slay the Black Witch. If told, perhaps nothing would happen right.

"Did you not hear me call?" Mrs Joy appeared at the foot of the attic room stairs. "Poor Angus looks quite eager to try his luck at tobogganing. Don't leave him waiting! The least you could do is to come downstairs." Mrs Joy had a new pinny and her hair was tied back with a familiar head scarf.

"Mum, that's Priscilla's head scarf!" Belle pointed to the florescent material on Mrs Joy's head. "Why are you wearing that?"

"Priscilla? Very formal dear, that name." Mrs Joy tightened the scarf to avoid getting her wisps of hair dusty from flour caked onto her cheeks. "Prissy left it behind. Strange, she just vanished. I left her scrubbing your grubby carpets, goodness knows what you children get up to, and I heard a rather loud commotion as I was taking a bath yesterday morning, just as you left for school with my tray full of Gemstone Delights. The bathroom window was open, so at first I thought it was those foxes again from outside, but when I peered through the glass all the roads and fields were empty, and I realised the voices were coming from up here." Mrs Joy glanced around as if she was to suddenly let on she too had discovered the time travel tunnel. "But when I got to the top of your staircase, the room lay empty. Only this head scarf discarded on the floor and a great black puff of soot from the grate. Most odd, Prissy had vanished, completely. Clean carpets like I never saw, mind. Anyway, come on, Angus is waiting." At a frazzled loss, Mrs Joy went back downstairs.

"Priscilla's using her time travel tunnel rather less cautiously now, isn't she? A bit too care-free." William was not sure whether to think that was a good thing or simply careless, but it was Priscilla after all.

"Hello." Angus seemed rather on edge, hopping about on the kitchen rug as the children tumbled into the steaming kitchen. "Fancy a ride?" He pointed to his sledge which stood perched up against the back garden fence. "Had it years, but never really tested it to its full potential."

"How on earth did you get that down from Scotland?" Belle asked. "I thought you were packed up with seventeen suitcases let alone have room for that thing?" and Belle pulled on her snow boots and tiptoed outside. "Brr! William, pass me my coat, it's freezing. This is just so strange." Belle lowered her voice so her Mother did not hear. "This *must* be Xavishum's doing. We can't possibly have blindingly white sun one minute and this thick freezing fog and snow the next. Look at the sky. The hue is deep purple, and the clouds, each passive cloud seems to be crumbling, subservient to that master black cloud growing and sucking the sky right in!"

Mrs Joy whistled in the kitchen. "Haven't you gone yet?" She pottered in the fridge. "It'll be dark before you know it! Come on, get out there!" And Mrs Joy brushed them all into the freezing night. Silhouettes they all became. "Ouch! Stupid pointed cabbages!" was all they heard.

Belle was right. Not only was the sky darkening in colour from a nice pale pink, but a sudden eclipse had an eerie presence. Belle glanced up, and what she saw made her take a deep lurid breath.

William passed Belle her pink fuschia coat. "Zip up," he said whilst he too pulled his furs around him. "Hang on, what's this?" William looked at the thick fur-lined coat Angus had passed his way. He looked bemused.

"I've grown." Angus stifled a cough and tried to look normal. "P...Mother asked me to pass it along to whom it may fit a while back, so I thought of you, William." Angus pushed out his chest and tried to force his height to more than it deserved. "You'll need it where we're going. Trust me, I know Arbrooth, it's bitter there sometimes to the extreme. Wrap up. We've evidently got harsh dealings ahead." Angus sounded so convincing it warmed Belle inside. She blushed. Angus noticed.

"Thank you! You are kind." Mrs Joy poked her head out from the kitchen, vapour and steam from her new courgette recipe melting the fresh white snow which had fallen on Angus's sledge. "You must absolutely invite your Mother and Father to us for tea. No buts, I'm so intrigued to meet them. Arbrooth, I do pride myself on the finer aspects of geography, but Arbrooth, I really must indulge in a new map. I don't recollect that one at

all! Can't wait to meet your Mother. Anytime suits."
And Mrs Joy slammed the door shut. She bustled back
to further triple stew her vegetables.

"You already have," Angus muttered. Belle frowned
at his low-voiced reply.

"Really?" Belle touched Angus's arm but he blushed
and pretended not to hear.

From the top of the hill the school at its foot looked
different, very different. The lingering austere black
cloud, growing larger and bitterly fierce, swung low,
and its shadow cast an enormous shape upon its victim.
The school looked diminished. Even old, perhaps? Even
morbid; its predator seeking her loathsome sanctity.

"Xavishum!" Angus cried, his eyes holding the
cloud's gaze before gradually rolling his stare upwards.
"Xavishum, she's not far now." But his words became
mingled with the deepest bloodcurdling growl the
children had ever heard.

"Vixonight!" Belle muttered. Her ashen-eyes,
perhaps now tinged with a little more hope, became
sunken.

Despite the moon still to rise, the looming sombre
cloud helped the Professor's cause. Its shining deep
silver-frosted layers cast beams, similar to the beams a

full moon would disperse, upon the man. It caused his clothes to rip and the hairs on the back of his neck turn to thick pointed bristles growing taller and further until they reached the crest of his head. Wild black eyebrows replaced the Professor's normal thin silver lines and his small mature greying eyes burned deep orange, perhaps red, in their bulging sockets. He rose tall. First his front legs departed the snowy road leaving deep footprints in their stead, followed by his muscular rear legs, primarily bent, grow tall and stealth-like. At the point where Vixonight looked like his height could not increase any further he turned his head vertically upwards, stretching his deep pink rough saliva-dripping nose to the darkening skies and let out the most excruciating roar imaginable.

"Grrrrrrrrrrrrrrrrrrrrrrr! Verona! *Sister!* I have the page! I have found the PAGE! The *Sorceror's Encyclopedia* has proved its worth, and now I have found the clearing, and within that clearing, I shall slay you soon. You had your chances to undo your spell, but now it is too late. Soon, your blackness will be disempowered, Xavishum will shrivel and Verona will be returned; a weak little girl with no claims and no enchantments."

Belle pushed her mittened-fists into her ears. William's mouth dropped open. But Angus, he sat taller and richer on his sledge; a crazed grin growing from one pink ear to the other, quite large William noticed compared to the pure small flakes of glistening snow that sat on top.

"William, the sky has a crack, look, right across its horizon, the sky is cut in two!" Belle gasped and clenched her brother's hand tighter. "And look..." Belle squinted into the crevice that the sky had created, the black abyss that was within, and saw that not only was the weather severe, but giant serpents, those serpents from before that William could understand, poked their long thick yellow-forked tongues through. Vixonight reached higher, his neck bridged steep to the skies, and his fangs snapping wildly at the serpents' hissing forked tongues. The serpents reached and retracted at each of Vixonight's slobbering and desperate bites in his pledge to defeat his sister, and regain his life.

"Angus, we need your sledge, quick!" and before Angus could say anything he found himself lying on the thickening blanket of snow. Belle had pulled the sledge from its vertical stance, and jumped on; her snow boots steadfast at the front, her voice wailing for the others to leap on behind as the serpents' vulgar and repugnant tongues flicked and lisped their way towards the children. "Go, Angus, go!" Belle yelled as all the threesome tugged then launched their way forward.

The sledge, at first, slid down Belle's steep cottage steps. Its passengers hopelessly gripped on. The sledge rope was hard and coarse, and Belle found that her palms became sore under the pressure, but she continued to keep a grip. Angus sat behind Belle, close to her hot shaking body, and the girl could hear a voice, Angus's voice, talking some strange utterances, utterances that were totally foreign to her.

"Praxitum, vroomba, grolumly, Verona." Belle heard Angus repeat time and time again, his tone increasing in volume and determination. It was all extraordinarily austere, far from human, and far from anything Belle had heard Angus produce from his quite Neanderthal-type character she knew. Belle tried to twist around to see if Angus was indeed alright, but her tight grip would not let her see.

"Angus?" Belle cried. "Angus, is that you?" But as soon as her questioning words left her mouth they were lost to the icy cold wind which whipped across her face and chilled her through. "Angus?" He did not reply.

"Look ahead! That black masterful cloud is far too low. And look, Mrs Lovett is gathering pupils for the Winter Sports Day. Is she mad?" Belle felt quite faint and bitterly cold. "Gracious, is she the goblin apprentice?" Belle whispered to herself. "It is, oh Angus, beware..."

The sledge pointed forwards, its wooden tip graciously carved with a horrible sharp metal peak positioned on the end. "That's neat, Angus!" William called. "Quite defined, are you sure this is just an old disused sledge from years back? Looks a pretty shapely thing to me. Awesome, in fact! I want one!" And as William spoke these words Belle thought the same. The far from battered offerings of a fun toboggan ride had the sudden feeling of agenda, even a pre-destined route whereby the sledge had a mind of its own. The wooden design boasted four perfectly chiselled seats deep within its body each with their own personal rope handle, but handles which could not possibly guide, only serve as grips from falling. The wood from which the sledge was carved matched exactly the old oak tree at school, and indeed had the identical grain of all their school chairs and tables. But what mystified William the most was the vicious metal tip leading the sledge forward.

"We're going pretty fast!" William held tighter to his rope. "I hope you know how to control this monster, Angus?"

"Well, not really!" Angus barked. "I've been meaning to test her out, but quite frankly the time has never ever been right."

"And now it is?" Belle cried back.

"Absolutely! We've been waiting years for this day. It's simply perfect!" Angus retorted. "Simply perfect, Belle. Hold ooooooooon!" Angus swung the toboggan sharp left and it's blindingly shining runners just kept on running smoothly, increasing in speed every second until Belle thought she was actually going to die. Hard hail stones smacked her in the face and she cowered down, hiding her head in her knees to avoid her skin freezing altogether.

"I hope they don't have this at the theme park!" Belle bawled into her legs tightly stuck together.

"I hope they do!" William cried. "I really hope they do!"

The toboggan slid on, vertically it seemed. Shooting down the steepest hill of all, Belle had to hold tight to whatever she could to stop herself from falling out head first. The night was close to sheer black and a deep howling resonated from somewhere.

Then, the toboggan shot in through an opening in the forest William and Belle had never noticed. "Roll off…now!" Angus tipped the sledge and as its passengers, hair on end and fingers frozen, fell to the snow-covered forest floor, the sledge halted before the old oak tree of the school grounds; school grounds which had begun to look depressingly dank and haunted.

"Oh, we're here!" Belle sounded surprised. "And what do you mean 'We've been waiting...?'"

"Ssh. We came the rear way to the clearing." A gravelly voice sounded from behind, and the group of strewn bodies, still lying in the crisp hard snow flung from the once speeding sledge, gasped and turned around. "The time has come." Vixonight's voice tone was low as he prowled with conviction behind the thick wide old oak tree. Blood dripped from his lips.

"Whose blood is that?" Belle whispered into the pointed werewolf's ear.

"The serpents' blood. All of them," was Vixonight's reply. The sky grew its darkest charcoal ever, deeper and darker. "Her servants are gone. Now for their master."

Belle continued to just stand and stare around until she finally gained courage to question the werewolf. "Professor Vixonight?"

"Ssh, Belle, the people are coming," the Professor's low voice rumbled, and sure enough Belle drew her eyes to the school's wooden doors which opened and a stream of children piled out led by Professor Vixonight. They looked down from their great height.

"Professor, it's you!" William spun around to face the werewolf and their wide eyes met. "Professor, blimey, are we in a time travel tunnel, seeing what will happen when Winter Sports Day finally arrives? Are we?" William was fuelled.

"No, William, not this time. Just me, I found the final chapter within the *Sorceror's Encyclopedia* to seek my revenge, and split myself between two places, indeed within the same dimension in time. I must be careful not to run into my other self, but this is the only way to slay her. Whether I live or I die, she must be slain."

"No Professor!" Belle tugged at the huge werewolf's fur. "I won't let that happen. You're not going to die!"

Tears rolled down her cheeks, but they froze immediately.

The werewolf roared. It regarded everywhere, his eyes always falling back upon himself leading his pupils outside, outside to gather around the old oak tree. The children shivered in the snow.

"Professor?" Belle tried again. "Professor, are you sure? Are you sure you want to slay your...your own sister?" She cowered a little knowing that the werewolf's reply would be an angered one.

"Of course!" the werewolf roared, causing a rift of snow to dislodge and tumble freely, gathering in size, down the icy forest hill. The werewolf crouched low as his Professor's body below looked up high. The Professor smiled.

"We have not much time," the werewolf grunted, and sloped off into the drifting fog. "Time is upon us to act." And he vanished.

William stared into the footprints left in the snow. The beast had gone and left him quite alone. Despite Belle and Angus by his side, William felt a heavy burden which had never lain quite so uncomfortably upon his shoulders. He turned to Angus.

"Why the sledge?" William's question appeared from nowhere. "Why the quite so dangerously metal-tipped sledge, Angus? Quite an impalement that sharp point, don't you think?" William spoke but did not know why his questions arose. He felt stunned. Belle just stared at her brother.

"Are you supposing Angus has his own agenda to slay the Black Witch?" Belle cocked her head in her brother's direction. "Well?" She looked at Angus.

"Nonsense, nonsense, it was just a bit of fun, this sledge," Angus replied, dipping his head whilst his eyes followed the beast's wildly immense marks in the snow down the hill to the gritty clearing. It looked dismal and foreboding.

"I don't know what came over me," William told Belle as he held her back. "I keep feeling responsible, and Angus seems to be quite...I can't seem to put my finger on it. He's just different, secretive, and not just moody old Angus anymore. Forget it, maybe it's me." But William could not help thinking Angus was somehow different today. "Wait up, Angus!" William dragged Belle through the forest branches, ducking as they lay low, the heavy snow weighing them down. But Angus had disappeared.

"Where have you been, goodness my boy, where *have* you been?" Priscilla's high voice, shaking as she spoke, sounded close by but neither William nor Belle could see through the fog.

"But Mother, I had to help, I just had to, and see, the tip is full, *her* spell book taught me the potion, Xavishum's spell book. I got so close to her Mother that I tricked her, I tricked the Black Witch Mother, and the potion that lies within this metal point will rid her of Anouka forever. Are you proud? I had to get away and help, and she never really trusted me, I'm sure of that, but I was her closest acquaintance."

William looked at Belle. "Who *is* Priscilla with? They've taken Angus's sledge. It sounds like that metal tip was full of poison. I can't imagine if that had got into the wrong hands. Imagine if Angus had touched it, I can't bear to imagine the outcome."

"You *do* fancy him, then?" William jeered.

"Get lost!" Belle retreated.

The fog thickened. William pushed snow-capped branch-upon-branch from his pale cold face and squinted his eyes to try and find Angus and the path. The snow continued to fall and it was not long before most of the tracks were completely covered. He could just about see the beast's footprints and those smaller ones inside which Angus had made. The voices had stopped. The beast had vanished. William and Belle stood alone, lost to the wood.

A sudden ball of dark emerald green lightning flooded the forest and William shielded his eyes, Belle's too, with the extra hanging cloth left draping from Angus's furs. The bright bolt lit up the trees for miles around, and it was then William saw her. For the first time, Xavishum's entire empowered body stood before him. As clear as the skies were black her presence was vile green. She rose in the clearing taller than the tallest trees themselves. And as William looked up all he could see was her grey wrinkled wart covered face peer back down. He felt small. He felt weak. Xavishum's chin jutted out so far that the wisps of coarse hair attached brushed with his icy cheeks, and her thin bony hands rose tall.

"I have you *all!*" Xavishum cried, her cackle causing tree branches to crack from their trunks and shower pointed icicles at her audience. "I have you all here now to sacrifice you, then I, Xavishum, will be righteous for eternity and Krook will reign!" Xavishum shrieked her commands and plucked Alyssa from the crowds below who became mesmerised in disbelief.

"Better late than never, Alyssa," Xavishum scorned and scraped her sharp black-pointed fingernails dangerously down the quivering girl's cheek.

"I knew you were a fake. I knew you would not bring these other three idiots to me. So, I came to you!" Xavishum tossed her dry tangled black hair up high, dust showering on to the floor. Myriad trembled behind Alyssa's skirt. "And you think you've won, do you? We'll see about that!" and Xavishum pulled a jewelled dagger from the crux of her belt of thorns. "Magic does not always need to be used. Brute force can prevail!" And she brandished her glinting weapon to the cloud causing waves of rain to fall instantly down.

"We will not give ourselves to you!" Belle stepped forward.

"Belle! Get back here!" William tried to grab her hooded-coat, failing as his sister launched herself towards the Black Witch's desolate clearing. "We have defeated worse! Your brother is our friend."

"Greer? That loathsome self-righteous failure of a man is here? Show yourself! I see. Hiding are we?"

Xavishum sounded full of contempt. "Still a coward? Show yourself, I say!"

"I'm here, you fool!" The beast stepped forward. "You were always so lonesome, sister, but you cannot redeem yourself now. Look, look at this audience, you cannot reign, you have not your wand." Professor Vixonight held his sister's stare. "You are indeed no worthy sister of mine." And the beast drew back.

William surprised himself with his boldness. His mind was still struck with an inkling of Priscilla's magic. It never seemed to rub off. William realised he could suddenly read Xavishum's mind. It was a confused soulless mind of unrequited love. He stared. He did not blink. Xavishum read the boy's mind, and he seemed to know. He recalled Vixonight's words.

"Xavishum will shrivel and Verona will be returned, a weak little girl with no claims and no enchantments."

As William held Xavishum's stare, her eyes entranced him. Her soul seemed suddenly lonely and her persona quite empty. William felt numb. He grasped Priscilla's wand high, enriched with power and magic to defeat the Black Witch's reign forever, but somehow, for some unknown reason he could not seem to fathom, the boy could not bring himself to slay the innocence, the lost unloved soul which cowered before him.

"Do it!" Myriad cried. "It's your only chance, William, strike her down!"

William tried to follow his bravado, but his heart pulled him aside. Flashes of his fall from the great old oak tree flooded back. Naribu, he had told him something that day, something he had cast to the back of his mind all along. *"Follow your dream......"* and this was what the *Sorceror's Encyclopedia* had as guidance too. He remembered.

William saw Xavishum crouched at his feet. Her eyes become more disenchanted each time Priscilla's wand trembled and quivered above her head. If her wand struck out, Xavishum would be impaled, never to be revoked.

"William, why are you dithering? Strike Xavishum now before it's too late." Belle cringed in terror, completely dumbstruck as to why her brother had even the slightest hesitation.

"William, YOU must!" Vixonight growled.

William looked across at the beast, and for the first time detected a sadness in his tone, perhaps a sadness which could be restored to happiness if William could only help.

"No!" William protested. "I can't and I shan't slay Verona. And *you* can't, can you?"

Professor Vixonight gnarled and his eyes burned so brightly William felt their heat from afar. "Professor, Verona is your own flesh and blood. Why not restore what you once held? Save her life and ask if she is saved. Ask that she undo the spells which Anouka does not deserve. You *can* do that?"

"I *cannot!*" Vixonight growled deeper, his conviction more determined than ever before. "Verona cast misery to so many in her path, and for that I simply *cannot* forgive. Strike her, William!"

"If you want that ending, you will have to strike her yourself then, Professor, for I cannot." But the beast just hung his bearded head low.

William, Belle, Angus and Alyssa shifted their feet, grinding the powdered snow further into the clearing as compact as could be. The black cloud floated upon them, the whole school watched in terror. Then a small speck appeared on the horizon. "Naribu," whispered William. The snowy owl grew closer. Then closer enough to whisper in the boy's ear.

"That is sure, plain as day, whole heartedly enough adjudication to make you head boy next term." Naribu implied. "Save Xavishum, she deserves a chance, do *you* think, William?"

"Yes," William whispered. "Yes, I do," he cried to the tallest of trees, and William slowly drew the wand away from the cowering ashen-faced witch and passed it back to her. "Verona, I shall save your soul if you restore all those who perished by your hand over many *many* years. If you re-enhance Anouka, cast Krook out of existence, I shall grant you a second chance. I shall know if you miss anything, we know one of your goblin accomplices is already at large. Reel that goblin in too, then you can rebuild your life with your brother. I could never have eternal hatred towards my sister, never." William winked at Belle, who in turn thought he had completely lost his marbles this time.

"I have no accomplice, not even one." Xavishum beckoned. "Not even myself did I really want to take evil this far, but the jealousy towards the love everyone held for my brother spiralled and this demonic side took over. I have no accomplice, of which I am aware, who is wholly true to me. There is none." Xavishum hunched further and further towards the thawing icy floor. "Verona would be honoured to return."

"We'll track down that elusive goblin, he can't be hard to find now Xavishum is shamed. He might just give himself up. We'll track him down." Angus nodded, his eyes darting about and quite distant from Xavishum's querying gaze, and he flushed to the very tips of his pointed ears.

The Return to Arbrooth?

"You will write, Angus, won't you?" Belle looked the Scottish boy in the eyes.

"Me? Write a letter? To a girl? Pen to paper?" Angus chuckled. "Yeah, sure, why not?"

"Liar," Belle smirked back. "We'll miss you over the summer, you being in Scotland. Do you think you'll return back here to school next term, what with your Dad regaining his work in Arbrooth?" Belle looked sad. William shook his head "We've never met your parents come to think of it, Angus."

"Me? You actually want *me* to come back and freak you out for another term? Taunt you with my anti-listening skills and be annoying right by your side for another school year? Surely not?" Angus chuckled again. He did look odd. "Anyway," Angus glanced around at all his fellows, but leant in towards Belle, so close she could feel his warm breath on her neck sending shivers down her spine. "Anouka needs me back again now. I belong there." Angus gazed into Belle's eyes. He saw her enquiring brow cast him over up and then down. His pointed ears which Belle had never once before noticed poking through his ruffled hair, stood up tall, and his freckles fizzed.

"You? You're the goblin? The Black Witch's apprentice? Angus, Angus I don't understand." Belle gawped.

"I had to get you involved somehow." Angus sat down on a rock. "My parentage goblin family could not defeat the Black Witch alone. I knew she needed four innocent victims to encircle around the old oak tree to empower Anouka and its outside for eternity, so I changed my look, became human to learn your respect, and sold myself, unknowingly to Xavishum as I cast a *Stay True to Yourself* spell on myself. I sold myself to the Black Witch. My family have been waiting, in fear, for years for the supposed mythical Xavishum to break her way free of Krook. We knew one day she would come..."

"...my sentiments, my sentiments, I knew that day would prevail too, despite all the grumpy comments." Priscilla spoke up and glared at Quindig.

"Yes, dear, you were right. Even when you're wrong, you're right." Quindig nodded, sufficiently reprimanded.

"Oh why, thank you, my dear." Priscilla tossed her pinkish hair provocatively.

Quindig rolled his eyes. "Such a pretence."

"My family did not have the means to defeat Xavishum alone, that's for sure. This *Sorceror's Encyclopedia* held the answer, and when one day I stumbled across your names, William and Belle, having prospered many times in Anouka, I knew I had to find you. Sorry I scared you by the pond that first day. Made you jump, didn't I?" Belle shunted him, and Angus lost his balance falling from the rock.

"Yes, you did. That was rather horrid. And the mirrored wall? Was that your doing too?" Belle asked, casting her mind back to every moment since meeting Angus that the goblin had appeared.

"Yep!" Angus replied. "I had to be believable. I had to make you think we really needed you."

Belle blushed. "Did Priscilla know, and the Professor? Did they both know you were the goblin?"

"No, no, fooled you all, didn't I? You see, I couldn't risk being found out. Even Alyssa was taken in. Priscilla and I, we were working towards the same cause, she wanted revenge for Xavishum banishing her ancestors years back, and Greer, Professor Vixonight, needed his youthful life back, rid of his sister's black art demonising him to being a werewolf forever. The serpents' voices revealed only Xavishum's bloodshed could ultimately set everyone free, release this terrible fear that Krook would reign and create everything all-powerful to her. Thanks for that, William."

"We did it," whispered William. "We banished Xavishum! We've slain her right here. Well, slain her ego." It was still hard to believe. But for Belle, Angus being the goblin apprentice was much more absurd. Slightly heart-breaking for her, she thought.

"I still can't believe that you, moody old Angus, brash and quite simply the least tactful and most inept, clumsy person I have ever met is not the Angus I've begun to..." Belle stopped talking. Angus looked at her. She wiped away a tear which she hoped nobody had noticed; especially Angus Moon. "I had actually, sort of, fallen for you," Belle took a step backwards. *What am I saying?* She felt shocked. She span around to see if Myriad was sniggering in a corner somewhere, shaking some sort of ridiculous devotion dust her way. *"You are totally not who I believed you to be. Typical really,"* Belle whispered silently.

"Your brother will be pleased, though," Angus smacked his hands together in a mocking tone. But faintly, and only into Belle's ear, he whispered, "and quite frankly I can stay Angus if you like? I'd quite convinced myself, in fact. I've fallen for you too, Belle." Angus touched Belle's skin, and he could feel she was shaking. "Gemstone Delight, anyone?" and the preposterous idea of breaking his teeth on Mrs Joy's baking lay a light-hearted blanket over the group.

"See you next term, back at school, then?" Belle coaxed Angus; she desperately wanted to keep her close friend just as she knew him. Plain old scrupulous, Angus Moon.

"Maybe, maybe, if your Mother hasn't broken my teeth with her baking, and my Mother, Prissy, I like that new name, if she doesn't come after me with a large spatula asking where have I actually been all this time?" Angus replied cockily, as he disappeared into the Old Oak Tree; a bright opening, a timeless light-side of Anouka with goodness knows what inside.

Belle could still feel Angus's touch upon her pale skin. "Don't forget your sledge?" she called, but glancing over her shoulder she soon realised it was not Angus's fingers upon her; just an awakening branch from the old oak tree where fresh green shoots were stirring, and baby acorns peeped towards the new born sun now causing dappled summer shadows to stretch lazily and carefree in its warmth. "Bye Angus Moon," Belle whispered. "Bye."

Philippa W. Joyner has worked professionally as a P.A. for two decades, but in 2013 she was inspired by her children's whimsical offerings and active imaginations.

The author originally grew up in Hertfordshire, and completed her studies at Bangor University, Wales gaining a B.A. Hons with Distinction in French and Theatre.

She currently resides in her chocolate box village in Kent at the foot of the North Downs with her husband, two children, and a multitude of wildlife.

Lightning Source UK Ltd.
Milton Keynes UK
UKOW02f1222290816

732UK00001B/3/P